The Lucky Ones

Also by Rachel Cusk

The Lucky Ones

A NOVEL

RACHEL CUSK

Fourth Estate

An Imprint of HarperCollins*Publishers*

FIRST U.S. EDITION 2004

Printed on acid-free paper

Library of Congress Cataloging-in-Publication Data has been applied for.

ISBN 0-00-716131-X

04 05 06 07 08 OS/RRD 10 9 8 7 6 5 4 3 2 1

Contents

'The firm compact little girls were not half so brave as the tender, delicate-looking little boys.'

Katherine Mansfield, *At the Bay*

The Lucky Ones

Confinement

Michelle had to get up with her now when she had to go. She was so big she bumped into things. Mostly it was four or five times a night but tonight it was more, eight times already and it wasn't light yet. She was stuck on her back and it was tickling down there. It was like someone was sitting on her, it was that heavy. She couldn't breathe lying on her back. Sometimes she felt she was being pushed out of her own body. It was like being killed, she thought, and then said sorry in her head for thinking it.

'*Shel*,' she whispered. '*I've got to go.*'

For a minute there was nothing and then she heard Michelle get up. She saw her looming around in the dark as if she was drunk.

'Mind out,' she said and Michelle swore. There was a thud and the sound of gasping. 'What happened?' she said.

Michelle was laughing. She was making gasping sounds and wheezing and Kirsty felt tremors start in her own stomach, the big muscles flapping and rolling upwards in waves and making her lungs hurt.

'Don't, I'll wet myself,' she said.

Michelle was rolling her over on to her side. She was still laughing; her arms were shaking and her hair danced jerkily over Kirsty's face. Kirsty stuck her legs out into the dark and Shel pulled her off the bed. Her feet made contact with the cold floor but her body was in a sort of landslide, things pouring downwards, and she reeled over after them, clutching at Michelle in the darkness so that Michelle staggered backwards. She thought they might just give and give until they went over but Michelle planted herself and pushed back against her. They were both shaking with laughter. She couldn't see a thing.

'I've wet myself,' she said. 'I'm wet at the back.'

Michelle got her under the arms.

'Hold it in,' she said.

'I can't.'

Water was coming out from between her legs; the spring of her bladder felt busted, the water just came out in a torrent and made a gushing sound on the floor.

'Christ,' said Michelle, 'you sound like a horse pissing.'

'I can't stop. Are you holding me?'

'Christ,' said Michelle.

'Shel,' said Kirsty, 'I can't stop.'

She smelled salt and half retched.

'It's your waters,' said Michelle. Her nails were digging into the tops of Kirsty's arms. There was pain, of a kind that couldn't be changed. She felt Michelle's hot flat body down her back.

'Sorry,' she said as the warm water flowed over their feet. She started to cry because she knew this meant the baby was coming. Michelle was pulling her back towards the bed. Her feet skidded and skated on the wet floor. She paddled in the air for a minute crying and then Michelle heaved her on to the mattress so that she was lying on her side and lifted her legs up after her. Her wet things were going cold. She shut her eyes and put her arms around her belly. Somewhere down the corridor she could hear women fighting in one of the cells in the dark. The baby travelled up through the core of her body; she held it, she embraced it inside. A fog of sleep hung in her head and she moved in and out of it. For a while she forgot where she was, and then she forgot that there was a baby, except that she felt more concentrated, denser. She felt more herself than she had for a long time, so that while sleeping she formed the idea that she was at home in her bedroom and that on the other side of her eyelids was her old wallpaper with the pattern of blue flowers; that her mum was downstairs making a cup of tea and that nothing had ever happened, nothing separated her from herself. She lay like this until the wetness around her pushed against her sleep and began to trouble her, so that she had to wake up and find out what it was. And then she saw the small room, bleak and grey in the dawn, and Michelle lying in a heap on the other bed, and her own stomach, which looked like big trouble, which looked like a bad dream. The light was like dirt. Doors were banging and people were shouting in the corridor outside. Shel had put a sheet down on the floor in the dark and it lay there twisted and sodden, seeming to replicate something in Kirsty's head. She closed her eyes again and this time like a fright she saw the house burning, with big branches of fire coming out of the top, and Julie and the children standing at the window with red behind them, waving.

'I couldn't hold it in,' she said to the warden, who was now standing in the smudgy light at the end of her bed. She couldn't sit up. Tiredness pressed against her face like a boot. The mess of her hair scratched at her forehead and cheeks.

'Clean it up,' said the warden, to her and Michelle both.

She went out and locked the door behind her.

'Have you got pains?' said Michelle. She was standing in the middle of the room. Her face was white and worried like a fist.

'No. I'm getting up.'

'I think we should tell them.'

Keys scratched in the door. The warden came back in and put a mop and a bucket down on the floor. Then she went away again.

'I'm not telling till I have to.'

The truth was she felt sick, the way she had at the beginning: it was the salty smell of the waters, a used-up dishwater smell with nothing sharp in it. It turned her stomach. And she felt like she was on the edge of it all, too, with the water gone, like you feel when you've jumped but haven't yet hit the ground, a kind of backpedalling in your head, a feeling of regret. She didn't feel any pain but she knew it was there. All this time it had waited in her body, quiet. It had waited, and now that the time had come for it to take her baby it just could, without her permission.

'I need my mum,' she said, starting to cry again, and Michelle didn't say anything. She was mopping the floor and putting the wet sheets in a bag.

'Come on then,' she said when she'd done.

She helped Kirsty into her big sweatshirt and the leggings with the panel sewn into the front. She tied up her trainers for her, squatting on the floor, breathing hard, while Kirsty stood there big and swaying, looking down like someone looking down from the top of a tall building and thinking about jumping. Then they went and stood by the door, waiting to be unlocked.

*

The prison was white, and when the sun came through the high-up windows the bars made strange, underwater shadows on the walls. You could never get any perspective with so much white: it made you feel small, and far from the edges of things. Kirsty would run her finger along the walls as she walked, wanting to get some texture, some purchase. The prison reminded her of something, some long-ago part of her life before things made any sense to her, when strange noises instead of words came out of people's mouths and rooms could suddenly turn upside down and she was a static point in a kaleidoscope of revolving angles and hours. Nothing had a beginning or an end then, and prison was the same. Her mum said that when she was little she used to carry around a bit of old blanket, and would rub the slippery, shiny edge between her finger and thumb. It was that edge, that border she was after. She liked the feeling of knowing where something stopped. She still sometimes looked around herself and wondered how that little girl had ended up in a place like this. Her mum would have said the same, but she could never bring herself to visit. Kirsty's mum always used to take her side in everything. She thought the best of her, until that became impossible. Now her mum just said that she didn't know. It was her auntie Dawn who did the talking.

'Webber!' shouted the warden across the refectory. She had the post; she shouted other names and women got up from their tables and went over.

'I'll go,' said Michelle.

'You not eating?' said Carol.

'I don't fancy it,' said Kirsty, staring at a piece of dry toast on her plate. *I want to die*, she thought. Her stomach was big and hot and tight. It pressed against the edge of the table.

'There's no room in you at the end, is there,' said Carol.

Kirsty remembered waking up one morning, when she was about ten, feeling so bad that she thought something about the world had changed. All her bones ached and she felt hot and cold and sick to her stomach, and she couldn't move, not one inch; and she lay there thinking, What am I going to do, how am I going to go on? It was as if kindness and understanding had never existed; as if she was all alone, and her life was a race, like in a dream, that something was stopping her from running. She had to go on but she couldn't go on, and there was trouble, trouble in her head and behind her eyes and trouble in the pit of her stomach. *You're ill*, her mum said when she came in, explaining it all, putting everything back in the right place in her head with just two words. Kirsty felt it now, that same confusion, except this time everything anyone said or did made it worse. Her leggings were wet at the crotch. The baby was coming. Her heart thumped in her mouth as she saw the faces of the other women, stiff with unhappiness and boredom and with never being looked at, faces that had lost their language.

'I carried small with both mine,' said Kay. 'They never believed me in the hospital, they kept trying to send me home. The second one was born in the lift.'

'They must have got a surprise when the doors opened,' said Rita. 'You squealing like a stuck pig with your fanny on show.'

'You're lucky it was quick, though,' said Janice. 'It isn't always quick like that. I was three days with my first.'

Kirsty could see Carol giving the others significant looks, but she didn't care, she wasn't really listening: they never meant anything to her, their stories, it just reminded her of what strangers they were to each other. You only tell people about your pain when you expect them to mind, but that was prison all over, everyone heard the echoes around themselves and then tried to pretend they weren't there. They knew you didn't care and they told you anyway. Michelle dropped a letter on the table in front of her and she opened it. *Dear Kirsty, You must be very near your big day by now and I hope you're managing. I know from personal experience how difficult those last few weeks are and cannot imagine how much more difficult for you, being so far from the people who love you.* Kirsty averted her eyes from the notepaper, which had little yellow flowers all around the edge. Dawn's writing was round and she pressed hard on the paper. All in a rush the smell and feel of her aunt came at her and even though it was welcome it was too strong, she had to put her hand to her mouth, thinking she would retch. She hadn't heard from Dawn in a while; she came to the prison when she could but it was a long way, and anyway Kirsty would rather Dawn spent the time on her mum. She started to fold the letter, thinking she'd read it later, because just now there didn't seem to be any room in her head for the words to go in, but as she was folding it she saw it said 'bad news' further down. *I don't like to be the bearer of bad news, especially at this difficult time, but I know Kirsty that you would want to know about your mother whatever the circumstances and I wanted to tell you before someone else did. Some men broke into her house Wednesday night, the night before last, and knocked your poor mother about and then set about breaking and destroying everything they could while she lay there helpless. She is in St George's now with two broken ribs and some cuts and bruises and one or two other things which I won't go into because you've got too much on your plate already. Needless to say your poor mother is in absolute shock, and she hasn't even seen the house yet, which is uninhabitable, having been defiled in ways I won't describe in detail here – suffice it to say these were evil and disgusting men with no respect for anything. What could have been the motive for such an attack, you may ask.*

Kirsty turned the page over. Her hand was shaking so that she couldn't hold it still. *Well your mother recognised one of the men as being Julie's brother Gary, who I've since heard is only a week out of prison himself and now I suppose will be going straight back in, which seems incredible because I remember him as being quite a nice little boy, but that was years ago and they all seem to go wrong some-how in the end round here, even the nice ones –*

When they heard her shout the other women looked around. They saw a girl with tears and mucus running down her face and her friends closing round her, and this was a sight which usually they ignored, prisoners and warders both, because people were always crying and showing their emotions here; there was nothing to stop them, nothing to soak up the feelings, except in this case the girl was nine months pregnant and one or two of the women wondered whether she might be starting.

Back in the cell Michelle had her arms around Kirsty. They were hairy, like a man's. Michelle was rocking her to and fro. It was important to Michelle that she was able to give people emotional support. Kirsty felt an urge to push Michelle away from her, to run from her squat, muscled body. At that moment Michelle's body just felt like another thing she had no choice about. Sometimes she felt that things between her and Michelle were real and sometimes she didn't. Prison was like that. You kept wondering what friendship could be worth in a place like this – they were all people other people wouldn't want to be around. What was the point of pretending they meant something to each other? She couldn't have said that to Michelle. Michelle was hard, but Kirsty knew you could kill her by saying that sort of thing.

Michelle was one of those people who had made something of herself in prison. She hadn't had much luck in her life, Kirsty could see that. It wasn't the kind of bad luck you had to be born on the Barrows, where Kirsty grew up. On the Barrows you were in it together; it was where you came from, like it or not, and although most people there didn't like it they made sure they had a laugh and stuck two fingers up at everybody else. Michelle spent most of her time in care when she was a kid. Sometimes they used to try sending her back to her mum, but her mum was a sad case, Michelle said, she drank and lived on the street half the time and only thought about getting herself involved with men. There was always some man around her mum was trying to be different for. What would usually happen was that Michelle would come back and the man would leave, until her mum started saying that every time Michelle came back she ruined everything, because she couldn't concentrate with Michelle around asking for things, at which point Michelle stopped coming back. Kirsty couldn't imagine having a mum like that. Her mum had never had anything to do with men, after Kirsty's father. Even the mums on the Barrows put the children first and the men second. Michelle was in prison for murder. She killed her husband. If you asked her what she was in for she'd say self-defence. Kirsty hadn't wanted to share a cell with Michelle, with a murderer. She'd cried silently with fear all the first night and didn't dare to get up for the toilet even though she was desperate. It never occurred to her that Michelle might feel the same thing about her, Kirsty, although as it turned out Michelle thought that everyone was innocent no matter what they'd done. She's just the victim of her circumstances, she'd say about this person or the other. It almost annoyed Kirsty that it didn't seem to matter to Michelle whether she, Kirsty, had actually done what they said she'd done.

There was a campaign for Michelle. All sorts of people wrote to her, journalists, politicians talking about women's rights. Kirsty didn't even know what women's rights were before she shared a cell with Michelle, but she knew now. There had been a television programme about her case, as Michelle called it. No one suggested that Michelle hadn't killed her husband: what they said was that she shouldn't have gone to prison for it. It didn't make any sense to Kirsty, until Michelle showed her the file of articles she'd cut out from the newspaper, which told what Michelle's husband had done to her. Michelle said to Kirsty once that she didn't particularly want to get out of prison; it was everyone else that wanted her out. Everything's the wrong way round in my life, she said. In here I feel free. If I was outside I would feel like I was standing still in time; I would always be stuck in that moment when I was in the kitchen holding the knife. I don't think I'd ever be able to progress beyond it. She told Kirsty about a man she'd read about in the newspaper, who had been sent to prison for burning down a barn, and on the day he'd been let out had gone back and burned it down again. I can really relate to that, said Michelle.

Michelle lifted weights in the gym and did prison courses and read books, piles of them, books about everything, books which always made life more complicated than it seemed so that it made your head hurt to think about it. To

Kirsty life was just something that went along; it was like a car that just went along carrying you with it and you didn't involve yourself in how. Michelle was different, she wanted to know how it all worked. Sometimes Kirsty thought that Michelle was disappointed in her. She'd got books for Kirsty about pregnancy, which Kirsty never read. She'd found out about Kirsty's case and how it had gone wrong and what the lawyers should have done but didn't, and although Kirsty knew that what Michelle said was true it didn't start her up like it did Michelle – it did the opposite, it made her feel tired and as if there wasn't any point to anything. Other times, though, she thought that Michelle liked having her to look after. It was Michelle who found her the new lawyer, Victor Porter, and Kirsty was interested then, because she recognised in Victor something simple that related to her own life, something material, namely a directly increased chance of her getting out of here. She depended on Michelle and she found her a bit much, one after the other, back and forth, but now that the baby was almost here it was more the first than the second. Michelle said things like, It's funny how we'd never have met if we hadn't both been in here, or, Every cloud has a silver lining, and Kirsty felt embarrassed.

So she let Michelle keep her arms around her, even though it made everything hurt, and the moment became one of those moments she sometimes had, when something real that had become something false became something real again, when she felt herself changing but she didn't know into who.

She knew Gary. He was a fat kid who used to smuggle himself into a group as if he thought the others wouldn't notice.

People hated him really, just for being a big prat, but he had a habit of doing ugly things, stupid things, to prove himself and so nobody could be bothered to have a go at him. He'd kicked her once in the playground at school, just for being Julie's friend and coming to their house. That was what he was like. She used to say hello and talk to him sometimes, and then he saw her in the playground one day and he came up and kicked her. He had this big smile on his face. When he did it she had the strange feeling that she could see inside his head, and what she saw was that he knew everyone hated him and that he hated himself more. She saw another person inside the person he was. She often got that feeling with men. That was before he got older and started getting into proper trouble. One day he pushed an old lady down the stairs of her flat and broke her legs. Kirsty wasn't surprised even though his family was. He used to visit that old lady, apparently, two or three times a week, and then one day he just pushed her down the stairs. They didn't know anything about the visits, the family, but it didn't surprise her because she knew about the other person in him. That was what gave him such nasty ideas. It was like he was taking it out on his other side. She couldn't remember what he was in for at the time of the fire. Julie wasn't talking about him by then. She'd got it into her head that he'd told the police about Shaun. She couldn't see how else Shaun had got sent to prison, although as far as everyone else was concerned it was a question of how he'd managed to stay out so long.

It hurt her to think about Shaun and Julie, gave her a pain right there high up in her chest. The baby didn't give her space to think about bad things. There was no room in her stomach for the feelings to happen. They got stuck in her chest, in her throat. She was mopping out the cells and trying not to think. Cleaning was all right. The others said she was lucky to get it, there were much worse jobs. She'd worried about the chemicals, what with the baby, but she liked being alone. Often she thought that if only she could be alone she'd work it all out. She was in a right mess today. She'd stuffed toilet paper in her pants for the water, which was still coming out. She was starting to have pains. Sometimes she forgot about it, she drifted back into that big ease with herself, that slow-dancing feeling she had about the baby, like they were holding each other close and there was no one else in the world. She was the only person in this prison who had something. The other women's bodies were flat and lonely: punishment brutalised them, wore them out, because there was no giving here, no life, just time being taken away. Because of the baby, Kirsty still lived in time. That was why she didn't want the baby to come out. The others looked at her like they were feeling sorry for her, like the prison cancelled out everything good about the baby, but for her it had been the other way around. They didn't know about her transfer. Victor told her not to talk about it. A lot of the women had kids of their own. They didn't want to hear about the baby unit. Kirsty wouldn't have talked about it anyway; she was scared of thinking about after the baby had come out, like it was bad luck.

She had to stop mopping and lean against the wall. Her heart was thumping, she wasn't so good. Things were a mess again, the way they'd been at the beginning. Her mind was coming alive, she could feel it, after nine months of sleep. It was like she'd woken up to realise that she was being pushed under water and drowned, like her whole time in prison had been a dream, and the reality, the real prison, was only just beginning. And like someone tired she tried to lull herself back, but she couldn't, she was awake and alert and feeling pain, bands of it across her stomach, an ugly cramping feeling inside that told her that today was a bad day. Don't worry love, her auntie Dawn used to say to her, we'll get you out of here, and Kirsty hadn't really heard her. It was as if Dawn was in one room of a house while Kirsty was in another; they were in the same region but they couldn't communicate, because Kirsty had locked herself away in her pregnancy while Dawn was still living with the fire and Julie and the kids and the police coming, and the verdict, which had sent Dawn's sister, Kirsty's mum, funny in the head so that she couldn't say anything any more except that she didn't know. Gary had hurt her mum, to get her back for what everyone said Kirsty had done to Julie. *He's only been out of prison himself a week.* There was a pain in Kirsty's stomach. This was a bad day.

'Your brief's here, girl,' said the officer, coming up behind her and giving her a fright so that she had to clutch her chest with her hand. He turned around and walked off. Kirsty propped the mop against the wall and followed him. The officer was walking too fast but she had to stay with him; she put her hand under her belly and leaned forward as she walked. They never told you here when your lawyer was coming. You could be anywhere, on the toilet, in the gym, and they'd take their time finding you so that by the time you'd got to the visiting room there'd only be ten minutes left. When she got there she saw the girl, Jane, sitting on her own at a table. She was looking round the room like there was something to see. All the other tables were empty, there was no one there. Kirsty's heart was thumping again.

She had to stop, slow down: she had the bad feeling again, seeing the girl, and she had to stop and give it time to wear off so that she could get control of it all and stop things going wrong. Standing in the doorway she breathed in, breathed out. The girl was still looking around with a sort of little smile on her face. Then she snapped her eyes around and saw Kirsty standing there, and she gave a funny wave and Kirsty had to go over.

'Where's Victor?'

'Hi, Kirsty,' said Jane. She said it like a teacher, or a receptionist, like she was determined to avoid trouble. 'How are you doing?'

'Why didn't he come?'

'I'm afraid Victor's not well today. He said to tell you he was sorry he couldn't make it.'

The girl was small with a sharp face. Her skin was pale and you could see the make-up on it, just a little, an expensive touch or two to let you know that she took care of herself. She wore a black suit jacket, tailored. Around her neck was a silver chain. She used to come to the prison with Victor sometimes, but she had never come alone before. Kirsty didn't like being alone with her. Suddenly she could see what the girl really thought of her. She could almost hear her thinking, *Thief, liar, whore. Murderer.* Victor wasn't like that; he brought out the innocence in her like a good quality. Jane wouldn't look at her stomach, her eyes kept hitting it and then bouncing off. Kirsty watched her, waiting to see her give the stomach a proper look, but she wouldn't. It hurt her that she wouldn't. She imagined her tick-tacking around her life in her little shoes, around London and her posh lawyer's office, fragile and efficient, controlling, doing everything the right way at the right time. Jane made Kirsty feel rough and tough and dirty, made her feel like punching Jane in the face.

'My mum,' said Kirsty.

'Yes, I heard,' said Jane. 'I'm so sorry.'

'Are they going to arrest Gary?'

'I'm afraid I don't know. You know what it's like at the Barrows.'

Kirsty did know what it was like: you got into trouble for everything that you didn't do and nothing that you did. She'd grown up thinking that the police were crooks, that judges and juries were bent, but now that she'd been through the system herself she understood that it was simply that other people thought the life they lived on the Barrows was bad, and that it didn't much matter what you were being accused of, if you came from the Barrows you were guilty of something. The man who'd stood up for her in court, the lawyer, even he'd thought that – he'd said as much. You've got to understand, he told her before she went in, that the jury are going to find some details of your lifestyle shocking. Shoplifting, drugs, sleeping around, the jury heard all about it, without anybody asking her if it was true. That was what had surprised her about what people like Michelle referred to as the justice system. Nobody ever asked you what the truth was. She used to go shoplifting with Julie sometimes, for things for the kids. They'd both been cautioned, once. And she never took any drugs, it was mostly the mums on the Barrows who did that. They'd pretend in front of the kids that they never touched the stuff, and then they'd pack them off to bed and all go round to someone's house and get wasted. They'd be up at seven-thirty all cheery to send them off to school and then the minute they were out the door they'd go back to bed to sleep it off. Julie used to say that you had to have a laugh sometimes if you had children, because you were always doing things for them and never anything for yourself. Kirsty spent a lot of evenings with Julie and her mates but she never took anything, not really. It would have upset her mum. And they loved their children, Julie and her mates. Kirsty didn't reckon that the girl sat in front of her now had ever loved anything as much as Julie had loved her children.

It was typical of Gary to pay someone back for something they didn't do in the first place.

'Are you all right?' the girl, Jane, was saying. She was looking at Kirsty but her face didn't change, except that you could see she thought she might catch something.

'Yeah,' said Kirsty, moving in her chair. A strap of pain had her round the stomach. She tried to breathe in and out.

'You must be nearly due.'

'Yeah.'

Her pain was loud in the quiet room. She kept thinking the warders would hear it. *Please*, she thought, *please, not yet.* She'd been there when Julie had Ian. Shaun had pulled him out because the midwife was late. He was good like that, Shaun, he wasn't afraid of women. The other men on the Barrows were nothing like him. He had this little shaggy pony, a mountain pony called Bonny, that he used to ride about on with his gun stuck down his trousers, like a cowboy. Nobody ever touched him. He was lucky. It was after Ian was born that he started with Kirsty, although he'd always liked her – he used to kiss her sometimes when he was pissed. Julie said it was all right with her, she'd got the baby, she said she didn't want Shaun bothering her. Shaun found them a flat up the road with a mate of his but Kirsty still spent most of her time over at Julie's, helping with the baby. She'd wanted to say this to the jury, that it was Julie she cared about, Julie and the kids, and Shaun was just a bit of fun. You have to understand, the lawyer said to her, that in the jury's eyes your relationship with Shaun Flynn furnishes you with a motive.

'On that subject,' said Jane, 'I'm afraid we're having difficulties getting you into the unit at Fordham.'

'What do you mean?' said Kirsty.

Jane was leaning right back, as if she thought Kirsty might attack her.

'The unit's full at the present time,' she said. 'I've been pushing but they've said they can't fit anyone else in.'

Kirsty stared at her.

'But Victor said—'

'You have to understand, Kirsty,' said Jane, 'that the unit is mostly for short-term offenders. In a case like yours they need to see compelling grounds for appeal if they're going to make an exception. Victor's doing everything he can to speed that up,' she continued, 'so the . . . the separation will at least be kept to a minimum. He's found a new expert to look at the fire evidence and we're getting some more information about timings—'

Kirsty was crying and the crying hurt her stomach and made it jerk so that tears streamed from her eyes and her face was all mashed up. The strap of pain pushed her against the back of her chair; she started to choke, coughing up gobs of mucus that spattered the table in front of them. She saw Jane spring to her feet, her arms flapping.

'Kirsty, please calm down, please try to calm yourself,' she said in a high-pitched voice, and in a blur Kirsty saw her signalling for the warder, and then the warder was there and Jane was gone and somebody had brought her a cup of tea.

'Have you started, love?' said the warder, kindly now, for things were so bad that they couldn't get worse; she was an object of pity instead of scorn, and she wailed and shook her head and the warder asked her if she could walk, and slowly led her back to her wing.

She lay on her bed in the cell and looked at the wall. Michelle sat on the other bed in a silence of solidarity. Since the prison had become too crowded they'd started locking them up in the afternoons. The other women complained about it but Kirsty had never minded, she liked the quiet and the chance to lie down. But that was because of the baby, because with something inside her to talk to, to love, the futility of being locked up in the afternoons had never really touched her. The baby had protected her, not just from the things that might have happened to her otherwise, the drugs and fights, the politics, the web of sex she'd begun to see around her, but from the greater imperative to rebuild what her sentence had knocked down: her value. This is what a person like Michelle did, she took a moral position. No one laid a finger on Michelle but it was hard work, not just the books and that but the caring, the effort she had to make to show other people she cared, because it warned them off, it made them uncomfortable and stopped them hurting her. Kirsty didn't think she'd be good at that, at proving herself. She'd always been looked after on the Barrows. Her mates used to laugh at her because she never got into trouble. They'd be laughing on the other side of their faces now.

I'll never get another chance, thought Kirsty, to be like I

was. She didn't know that that person had been any good anyway. It was funny how the system had brought her into the orbit of people she would otherwise have known nothing about, people who thought she was disgusting or tragic or bad or a victim or *immoral*, which is what the judge had said, as if he'd never met anyone like her in his life. Even Victor thought that, for all she knew. He had a big house in London and another 'in the country', not on the Barrows, that was for sure, although he always used to say how beautiful the countryside was round there, as if this might have been something they could have chatted about. *Quite charming, isn't it?* He had two children and his wife wrote a column every week for some big newspaper. The column was about their family life, about bringing up the children, the ups and downs. Kirsty wanted to know if she got paid for it and Victor said that she did, very well, and Kirsty nearly split her sides. Do you think I could get paid for writing about family life on the Barrows? she said to him, as a joke, and he looked sad and said probably not and it was just another one of those things in life that were the wrong way round. I wanted to be a writer, she told him, when I was little. I wanted to write love stories. I wouldn't write about the Barrows if you paid me.

The pains had stopped. She lay on her side with her arms around the baby in her stomach. It was Shaun's baby, and all along she had thought that this meant it would be a lucky baby, like Shaun was lucky, just as she had secretly thought that Julie and the kids weren't dead, they were just hiding somewhere, waiting to come back. She was with her mates when they heard about the fire, it was a hot night and they were up on the hill completely pissed and someone had come running up and said Julie's house was alight and they had all gone down and found Shaun outside it with a black face and clothes from running in trying to get them out. Smoke was pouring from the windows, there was no fire any more; just in the time it had taken them to come down the house was burned out. They're still in there, Shaun said, and they'd all of them clung together and cried. Shaun said he'd gone down the road to see someone and when he'd come back the house was burning. They sat up all night trying to make sense of it. It was me they came for, Shaun said, over and over again, shaking his head. It was eight months before the police called round at Kirsty's. She was still seeing Shaun, because it was like being close to Julie and because he needed some comfort and because she hadn't known she'd had anything to hide, and then it turned out that two of her mates had said they'd missed her for ten minutes or so on the hill that night all those months before, and though Kirsty was sure she hadn't gone anywhere she had to say she couldn't remember, because she couldn't, she was too pissed and it was only seeing the fire that had brought her to her senses. The police said the person who started the fire had broken down Julie's front door and poured petrol on the hall carpet, and Kirsty said, Well I couldn't have done that, could I, Shaun's got it reinforced with bars on the inside, but no one seemed to care about that.

Her mother had always said to her that she could be whatever she wanted. Don't mind what other people think, she said, just be yourself. She read this kind of thing in old magazines at the doctor's surgery. When her mum had moved to the Barrows it had been a new estate, with gardens and flowerbeds and a little shop on the corner. She'd moved there from the town when Kirsty was a baby, thinking it would be a nice quiet place for them to live. Kirsty could see now that her mum had been going downhill even before the business with Julie. It was the changes on the Barrows, half the houses burned out, the gardens gone now, the shop boarded up, and the men – the men were like animals, always fighting, walking around in broad daylight with guns and knives, they were so bad the police didn't bother to come up there any more, they reckoned they'd leave them to it. 'Lawless' was the word for it, the word they'd used in court, except that there seemed to be plenty of laws suddenly, in there, in that courtroom. The women held the Barrows together. Kirsty's mum wasn't one of them, she didn't belong in a place like that, but people ended up in the wrong places all the time through no fault of their own. No one in her family had ever got into trouble with the police. Dawn lived in a nice house in town and her husband had a job at the car plant, but Kirsty's mum had fallen pregnant with Kirsty at seventeen and whoever her dad was hadn't wanted to know. She'd go and live with Dawn now. There was a room there for her, now that Dawn's Suzanne had married and left home. Kirsty wasn't going back to the Barrows either, not if she could help it. She'd go somewhere else and make a new start with the baby.

'You all right there,' said Michelle from the other bed, and Kirsty woke up, because she'd half gone to sleep thinking about the baby, and finding a flat for them to live in and maybe training to get a job and she'd forgotten where she was; and waking up to see that she was still here, in the prison, it struck her properly for the first time that she was going to be in here for ten years and she wouldn't see her baby until she was ten, a grown-up girl, and that all those looks she'd been getting from the other women, the silences in front of her and the funny way they met each other's eyes, were to do with that, with what they knew and she didn't about the way life went, about what happened once you'd let yourself get into a place like this, about things going from bad to worse. What does it matter? she thought. She made herself small. For a moment she herself was the baby and the child inside her took on a strange authority, the primacy of an unlived life. It seemed to her then almost as if the baby had the power to free her from herself. In this small room where the light behind the bars wore the sad pallor of a winter afternoon, of a day slipping by unlived, untasted, in this place where everything existed in a single dimension of fact, it was a miracle that this transference was possible. A point of pain pricked her belly and then spread slowly, unstoppably, like a burn.

'Just breathe,' said Michelle. She was standing by the bed with her hand on Kirsty's hair.

Kirsty took the pain like a lash. There would be another, and another. It had the measured, deliberate cruelty of punishment. It was real, illicit, meaningful. She felt summoned from her anonymity. Suddenly she was full of fight. She hoped it would kill her.

'And again,' said Michelle. 'Keep breathing.'

The pain knocked the wind out of her and sent her breath pressing against the top of her head. It felt metallic, abstract. She vomited, hotly, bitterly, on the sheet. The lights had come on: electricity was burning around the corners of her eyes. She turned her head and saw dark behind the cell window. There were other people in the room. It was like kicks to her stomach now, she saw it coming, felt the contact, felt the pain go all the way in. She shouted back at it, noisy and vicious. Michelle was talking in her ear and Kirsty had to come back to hear what she was saying, so that the next pain took her by surprise and floored her.

'They're taking you in,' Michelle said. 'Kirsty? They're taking you in now.'

Kirsty roared and shook her head, she wasn't going anywhere, she had to stay here and fight because otherwise she would lose, it would get control of her, and when she saw the two policemen coming across the room at her she windmilled her arms, slapping them, and they called her a cow and slapped her back, and it was because she'd hit them that they decided to cuff her before they picked her up one leg and one arm each and carried her out along the corridor. She bellowed and kicked hard with her legs as she went along, while the ceiling jerked around above her, and something about the ceiling, hard and white with big naked lights, unmoved, made her start to cry, and she closed her eyes and let the water run out of them.

In the police car the smell of plastic made her gag and one of the policemen made a squealing noise and shied away from her across the seat. She vomited over her own clothes. The handcuffs were a bar of pain, they conducted it from her stomach all around her body. When she shut her eyes she saw red. There was no room in the back of the car and when the next pain came she scrabbled around, trying to find space and purchase and needing to put her legs up before it came.

'Jesus fucking Christ,' said the policeman.

They went round a corner and she fell across his lap and gripped at the black cloth of his trousers with her nails, because she had to hold on to something so that she could push. The pain was different now, it was all down below, it was like a big rock in her that made her want to eject, to peel back from it. She still had her leggings on. She got herself upright and leaned against the policeman's shoulder with her chest so that she could get at the leggings.

'She's fucking having it!' shouted the policeman.

'Hold on, love,' shouted the other one driving.

'Stop the fucking car, she's fucking having it!'

This was what she wanted now, to feel herself dismantled, to be broken up. Inside her head it was dark; the lights of her mind were out. She bellowed and bore down. The world seemed to her dispersed, disintegrating: it was all suffocating surfaces and discord, the crazy lights from the road, the jumble of colours and shadows and noises, and herself webbed in it, as if she too were being left behind, cast off with everything that was tired and dirty and lived, that could no longer be redeemed.

'We're on the roundabout at Founthills Road,' the policeman said into his radio. 'Up on the verge by the city-centre turnoff. You're going to need to be fucking quick, though.'

The rock was lodged between her legs. It was moving with the stately violence of a glacier. She waited for the pain and then pushed again, in spite of what it meant for her, because she knew with that push it was going to rip her apart and it did, the pain was throttling, it was murder that modulated into the consciousness of something new, a new fact, a development. She was kneeling up against the back of the seat with her face pressed into the scratchy plaid fabric. For a moment everything was quiet and still. She put down her hands together and felt the head. It was hot and wet, protuberant, like a question. She touched it gently all over. Then she twisted her wrists so that the handcuffs hung down below and pushed the baby into her hands.

Outside the car the policemen were silent. She smelled

cigarette smoke. The baby had cried a little but now she was quiet against Kirsty's chest. Her skin was streaked with blood and her hair was plastered against her head. She made little movements. Kirsty raised her eyes and saw through the back windscreen of the car the great black loop of the roundabout ablaze with lights. The traffic flowed around it in a circuit so ceaseless that it seemed almost to be a living thing, incorporating, casting off, until you picked out one car, watched it hesitate in its tributary then join the perennially circling heart, and you thought it might just stay there, your car, going round and round for ever, but it didn't, its little yellow light started blinking on and off and with inexplicable sorrow you watched it veer steadily, inevitably away, on to another road, going elsewhere.

The Way You Do It

The little town, high in the eastern Alps, was reached by an old cog railway that wound up and up through steep valleys, and as it neared the top the incline was so great that the carriages made a sound of lamentation, a long shriek that went echoing down the silent snow-filled chasms below.

'I don't even know what language we're supposed to be speaking,' said Lucy.

'German,' said Christian.

'Oh,' said Lucy. She set her mouth in a line. 'It was French at the airport. I could just about cope with French.'

Darkness had fallen since they'd left the station. Squares of electric light from the windows laid themselves over the black ground outside, illuminating a thick, dirty crust of snow running alongside the track. Clumps of fir trees receded in penumbral waves, appearing from the lit carriages to be journeying in a mass towards an unseen shrine.

'They all speak English anyway,' said Christian. 'It's the language of business.'

'As opposed to love,' said Josephine, who was sitting opposite him. She folded her arms, leaned her head back on the seat and closed her eyes. In repose her beauty was as pale and effortless as that of a statue. Just then the train entered a tunnel and the wailing of the tracks hammered loudly at the window, as if in protest, or clamorous invitation. The incline steepened and a shade passed over the faces of the six people inside the carriage.

'Let's hope the brakes work,' said Lucy. 'Or whatever it is.'

'It's a cog system,' said Jane sharply, 'isn't it, Tom? I don't think it can go backwards. Tom, the train can't just slide back down the track, can it?'

'Not unless the man lets go of the rope,' said Thomas.

'Don't!' shrieked Lucy. Her eyes were small with alarm.

'Did you say you'd been here before?' said Josephine.

Martin nodded and turned to look out of the window, but it was now so dark that only his reflection came to meet him, a fleshy obstruction that mirrored his movements.

'Once? Twice?'

She splayed her hands impatiently palms-up towards him, as though he were refusing to pass the ball of conversation. Josephine was an old friend of Jane's from university. He had only met her that morning, at the airport. He felt like he had met her before.

'A few times.'

'I get it,' said Josephine, with an air of satisfaction. He noticed that her eyes were as black as her hair. She wore gold hoops in her ears, like a gypsy. 'You were one of those children, summers on daddy's yacht, Christmas in the chalet—'

'It must be nice,' interposed Lucy hopefully, 'for you to have wanted to come back.'

'This is it,' said Martin, standing up to lift down the bags from the luggage rack as the train slowed and crept into the station.

The station was quiet and cold and Martin walked slightly ahead of the others along the platform and out into the street. The thin dry air entered him; the little town was lit orange against the mountain's immense blackness. The freezing sky was low and cloudy, a presaging of snow. On every side darkness fell away, cascading downwards into space. Stout, muffled figures slowly walked the pavements, their heads wreathed in the steam of their breath. The others came up behind him with their bags and stopped where he stood. Looking down, Martin noticed that Christian was wearing cowboy boots, shiny and high-heeled with pointed toes that curved upwards.

'I've got all the details here,' said Jane. 'The rep's going to meet us at the apartment.'

She spoke in what Martin thought of as her lawyer's voice, although he hardly ever heard her speak in any other way. She had a wad of papers and a map. They followed her across the road and up a narrow gritted sidestreet, which led them quickly out of the centre into a wide, slushy expanse where big new apartment buildings stood at conversational angles to one another. They were built chalet-style and clad in pine. They hadn't been here the last time Martin came. Although some of the windows were lit, the development had a ghostly air of desertion. Usually Martin stayed at a small hotel in the centre, where men in salopettes with mournful eyes and drooping moustaches breakfasted silently in the sepulchral dining room. He had stayed there last year, with Dominique. She had refused to go down and eat with the silent men, even though breakfast was included in the price of the room.

Their apartment was in the basement of one of the buildings. The rep wasn't there but the door was unlocked so they went in. It was so cramped that the six of them could hardly fit into it with their bags. They waited for the rep to come and sort it out but when she arrived, a tanned German girl in tight white clothes, she opened her eyes wide and said, No, there has been no mistake, this is for six people. She opened a cupboard and a bed fell out of it and thumped to the floor. There were two tiny rooms off the sitting room, one with a double bed and one with bunk beds.

'We're not three couples,' Jane explained. 'We're six people but we're not three couples. Do you see? I said six, not three sets of two.'

'What difference does it make?' shrugged the rep, pouting her lips. 'Two here, two there and two there.'

'We're two couples,' said Christian loudly. 'And two single people. Four of us together and two not together.'

'Josephine?' said Jane. 'What do you want to do?'

'Whatever,' said Josephine. 'I don't care.'

'If you don't want to sleep together,' said the rep, 'you have boys in there, girls in here.' She shrugged again. 'It's up to you.'

'And one couple together,' said Jane consideringly. 'That's not really fair on the other couple.'

'Oh, we don't mind,' said Lucy. 'We don't mind, do we, Christian?'

Christian didn't reply.

'It's up to you,' repeated the rep, looking at her watch.

'Are you sure?' said Jane.

'It's fine,' said Lucy. Her face was bright red. She sounded out of breath. 'Honestly.'

They walked up and down the main street looking for a bar. The street was lined with the expensive, well-lit windows of boutiques, which showed tableaux of leather and gold and fur. Twice they passed Martin's little hotel; he glanced at its small, modest entrance without saying anything to the others. Looking up he saw the window of the room on the top floor that he and Dominique had stayed in. The lights were on; there were people in there, and in some strange way it seemed to Martin that it was himself, that he and Dominique were in there, eternally living moments of their past. He had experienced those moments it seemed to him now unconsciously; it was as if his awareness were something of very recent provenance, a new blight. He could not think without knowing that he was thinking, could not be without this sense that he was witnessing himself from a critical distance. When had his life, as something lived, ended? It struck him that time was perhaps no more than the passage of certain feelings. What separated him, he thought, from the days he had spent in that room, on the other side of that window, was not time but the fact that his feelings for Dominique seemed to have changed.

'Let's go back to that place further down,' said Jane. She had her hands in her pockets and the hood of her jacket up. Its fur trim made an incongruous frame for her narrow, pointed face. 'Tom? What about that first place we tried? Why don't we go back there?'

'I'll see you there,' Martin called to the others. 'I'm just going to make a phone call.'

He crossed the street, and standing in a freezing booth he dialled the number of his London flat. The machine was on; he guessed Dominique must already have gone to bed. He wondered if she had the baby in with her. He left a message, speaking carefully and quietly, laying the words gently over the darkened rooms and their sleeping forms as a protection against loneliness and the night. He inhabited those rooms

31

momentarily like a ghost. Then he was back, his heels ringing on the frozen pavement, his breath coming in white puffs, hurrying down the street to find the others.

'My granny wanted to die in Switzerland,' said Josephine. 'There was some hotel on Lake Geneva she had her eye on. She had all the brochures.'

'The ultimate holiday,' said Christian. 'The last resort.'

'She never made it,' said Josephine. 'My mother said for that money she'd look after her herself. My granny died on the spot. If you knew my mother,' she added, lifting her glass to her lips, 'you'd understand her point.'

'I'm sure it wasn't just about the money,' said Lucy disapprovingly. 'I think it's right to offer to care for your parents.'

'Oh God,' said Christian.

'The problem is that one of you usually gets lumped with all the work,' said Lucy.

'I'm not going to live with my children when I'm old,' said Jane. 'I think it's really selfish.'

Martin opened his mouth to tell Jane that she didn't have any children and then shut it again.

'I've always known that it would be down to me,' Lucy was telling Christian. 'My sister,' she added, addressing the group, 'doesn't really get on with my parents.'

'I had a job in a care home one summer,' said Josephine. 'They just used to sit, day after day, staring at the television or looking out of the window. Nobody ever came to see them. Half of them didn't even know what their names were any more. It was as though nothing they'd done in their lives mattered. I used to talk to them and they would remember things about the past, sometimes really interesting things, and you'd realise that thirty or forty years earlier they'd all have been completely different, but now they were all the same.'

'That's really depressing,' said Jane brightly, looking around.

The bar was clad in pine from floor to ceiling. It was crowded with people speaking German and French, who looked large and loudly coloured. The claustrophobic interior seemed to erase the memory of proportion, so that Martin could no longer remember the size of anything, the mountain on which they were perched, the infinity of space and darkness above and below them, nor how far he was from his city, his house and the rooms in which he lived.

'It's funny how having children has made me see my own parents as much more vulnerable,' said Lucy. 'My sister still sees them as the enemy. I'm sure that's because, in an important way, she hasn't grown up.'

'How's Dominique doing?' said Jane.

'She's fine.'

'How's the breastfeeding going?'

'Fine. Great.'

'Did you say she's got her mother staying with her this week?'

'That's right.'

'She must have really wanted to come,' said Lucy, her face screwed up in sympathy as though watching someone in pain.

'You've just had a baby,' Josephine stated, tagging on to their conversation.

'Yes,' said Martin.

'Congratulations.' She said the word with a slow, incomprehensible smile. He felt imprisoned behind the barrier, the fact, his life had become. The women were staring at him, and stupidly he rubbed his face as if there were some mark on it at which they were looking.

'Thanks.'

'It must be really difficult,' said Josephine, 'for you. You know, do I get on with my life, do I stay at home being supportive—'

Martin looked at Thomas, who was sitting next to Christian at the other end of the table arranging matchsticks around his bottle of beer. Thomas was his best friend, but he hardly saw him any more.

'Two moves,' said Thomas, 'to get the bottle inside the box. Without moving the bottle.'

'Without moving the bottle,' said Christian.

'Ten seconds,' said Thomas.

'Wait,' said Christian. He was leaning forward with his face close to the matchsticks. A vein stood out on his forehead. 'Just wait.'

Martin stood and took his beer down to the other end of the table. Josephine glanced at him as he went, and out of the corner of his eye he saw her lean over and say something to Jane.

'The way you do it,' said Thomas, 'is like this.'

He moved the matchsticks. Christian studied them, his face turning red.

'Oh,' he said. 'I wasn't even close.'

'What's the forecast?' said Martin, sitting down next to Thomas.

'Hot,' said Thomas. 'Very hot.'

He stared insinuatingly at Josephine, who was still talking to Jane, and smirked. Martin and Christian looked at her too.

'How's the nipper?' said Thomas.

'Fine, I think.'

'I don't know how you did it,' said Christian. 'Coming away on your own. The only place I get any time off from the twins is at work. This is the first time we've left them.'

'Dominique's got her mother there,' said Martin.

'I really miss them, actually,' said Christian. 'I couldn't wait to get away, but it feels strange being without them. And yet I know that the minute I get back I'll want to get away again.'

Christian's face turned red. The blood rushed up and down beneath his tight, transparent skin. He was strangely pretty – he had a pink, curving mouth and his eyelashes were long and curled, like a woman's. Thomas had turned around in his chair and was talking to a ski instructor at the next table.

'Snow's on its way,' he announced, turning back to them. 'Hey, Jane, snow's on its way.'

'That's great,' said Jane. She pursed her lips and folded her arms on the table, as though she had arranged the snow previously and was glad, but not surprised, to hear that it had arrived.

'Can you ski when it's snowing?' said Lucy. 'I've only been skiing once,' she explained to Martin. 'Years ago.'

'It comes back very quickly,' said Martin.

'I fell over,' said Lucy, 'and skidded all the way down the hill into one of those tow lifts. Somebody's ski went right into my head. I've still got the scar.'

She lifted back her heavy brown hair and searched among the roots with her fingers. Martin saw the dead whiteness of her scalp, speared with swarming dark wires of hair.

'Why don't we do the season,' said Thomas, nudging him.

He spoke as if confidentially, although was loud enough for everyone to hear. 'Get a job in a bar and ski all winter. Grow moustaches.'

'Thanks,' said Jane. 'While I do eighteen-hour days at Browning's.'

'Is that your new job?' said Lucy.

Jane nodded.

'I'm sending her to the City,' said Thomas. 'It's a new kind of justice. Skiing for all.'

'I didn't know you were leaving your job,' said Martin.

Jane's job had always surprised him. Every day, on his way to work, he crossed the littered junction and passed the bleak concrete building where her firm had their offices. The building had the battered, defiant appearance of a trench. He often saw Victor Porter, Jane's boss, on the news. He looked like a soft man. Jane wasn't like that at all. She was as hard and sharp as a sliver of glass.

'I got tired of it,' said Jane. 'It was all so squalid.'

'Browning's is a big firm,' said Christian.

'You just spent all your time worrying about people,' said Jane. 'They'd come into your office wanting to offload their terrible lives on you. And half the time you couldn't make any difference, you know, even if you got them off the odds were still stacked against them. They still had to go back to these awful lives. They'd come in with this look on their faces – you know, make it better. And I couldn't. In the end I couldn't take it. One day I just thought, actually, life doesn't have to be like this. It's allowed to be fun, you know?'

'I can really understand that,' said Lucy.

'What are you going to be doing?' said Christian.

'Securities,' said Jane.

'Big bucks,' nodded Christian.

'It's so hard, isn't it,' said Lucy, 'to stick by your principles. All the things you think when you're younger. Like before I had the twins I was absolutely certain that I wouldn't educate my children privately, but now, whenever I walk past our local primary school I get this sort of pain in my stomach at the thought of having to send them there one day. It looks like a remand centre. They don't make it easy for you, do they?'

'A teacher there got blinded in one eye,' said Christian. 'By a six-year-old girl.'

'A six-year-old girl,' repeated Lucy. 'Another friend of ours had to take their son out because he was being so badly bullied. Apparently he was the only child in the class whose parents lived together. The other children thought he was strange.'

'I feel bad for my boss,' said Jane. 'He's such a sweetie. But he's leaving anyway. I think he's ill, actually. He hasn't been in the office much.'

'It obviously got to him too,' nodded Lucy.

'It'll all change completely when he goes,' said Jane. 'He was the one who kept the miscarriage agenda going. So in a way, it's a good time for me to leave.'

'Isn't it his wife who writes that family column?' said Lucy.

'That's right,' nodded Jane.

'I like that column,' said Lucy.

'Skiing for all,' said Thomas, raising his beer bottle.

They walked back to the apartment. It had started to snow. The flakes fell on their hair and coats like the soft touches of ghostly fingers. They walked with muffled footsteps.

Thomas ran ahead and lobbed a snowball back at them and the women shrieked. In the apartment Jane and Thomas disappeared into their room, shutting the door behind them. Their voices, low and indistinct, could be heard on the other side of it. Martin sat on the camp bed reading a book while Josephine and Lucy and Christian went in and out of the bathroom with their sponge bags. When they had finished he got up and locked himself in the bathroom. He looked at himself in the mirror in the harsh electric light. When he came out again the light was off. He could see the mound of Christian's body in the other bed. The women were in the room with the bunk beds. A bar of light showed beneath the door. He felt his way through the room and lay down.

'Goodnight,' he said.

He woke later to an angled, unfamiliar darkness. His mind inhabited it with a rudimentary life. When he thought of his wife and child he felt like something that had been discarded from his own existence, a component, like a wheel that had come loose and spun away. He slept and woke again, startled, thinking that he could feel the baby down by his feet, burrowed like a warm worm in the bedding. He threw back the covers in panic. Later he woke again and swept the floor by his bed with his arm, thinking that she had fallen out. Occasionally Christian turned over and the sound of the rustling bedclothes was so close that Martin's heart bolted insanely with fear. Then he would lie awake for a while, oppressed by the room's smallness and dry air. He felt amputated and yet strangely continuing to exist, to grow into the new grooves of minutes and hours like some kind of botanical experiment involving the plotted torture of sunlight.

In the morning he got up and dressed before the others were awake. He manoeuvred himself through the cramped maze of furniture. As he opened the apartment door Christian's arm flailed up from beneath the bedclothes. Martin surfaced into the freezing, sunless glare of the street. The sky was white. The air was thin and coldly drenching. It seemed to form crystals in his mouth as he breathed. He bought a croissant from a bakery and ate it as he walked to the lifts. The streets were already full of skiers, streaming in from the tributaries of sidestreets. Their heavy boots thundered on the pavements. He fed himself into the crowd and was borne through the barriers and into a lift. As they ascended he looked around. The sight of the mountain in daylight was like waking from the confinement of a dream. It began to show its peaks and crevices, its colossal flanks, as the lift rose higher. Blue-green waterfalls hung in frozen cascades down rock faces. Trees smoky with frost stood in clouds above the snow. There were children on the lifts ahead of him. Their parents sat to either side of them, as erect as sentries. His own daughter was three weeks old. He imagined them skiing together, when she was older. He had the feeling that this was the correct thing to imagine under the circumstances, but it didn't really mean anything to him. He felt as though he was walking further and further out, on a tightrope that led nowhere, so that every step he took was part of the retraction he must make to get back to where he had been. The thought of his daughter filled him with spurts of nervous warmth, and with the alarm of someone who has dropped a plate and is watching it in the last seconds of its wholeness, before it hits the floor.

The snow was good. Martin knew it through the first

contact of his skis. The cloud had cleared and the sky was visibly deepening with blue. He could see the massive, sculpted peaks of other mountains. Their forms seemed to recall the world in a primitive state, in the swirl of creation. Other skiers shot by him, their bodies straight and graceful, swaying from side to side with the precision of metronomes and then vanishing in a spray of powder. He skied at first cautiously and then fast as the rhythm came back to him. By the end of the first run his head was cleared of thought. It was like illness lifting from the body. He took the chair back up to the top. Suspended above the piste in the sun he was vacantly happy. Other people hung around him in the air, huddled, anonymous, like machines in a state of pause. He skied down again and came back up on the lift. The third time, halfway down, he forked off to the left where the piste divided. The slope faced a different way here. Large, bald blisters of ice shone through the snow. He went down a gully and skidded out the other end to find himself at the top of a broad, icy wall. People were going down it in big curves, slipping metres at a time. He stopped to consider what route he would take through them. Just below him a woman had stalled on her skis facing the wrong way, towards the edge. She was bent over with her legs apart and she was clawing the air with her poles, which waved about forlornly like antennae. While Martin watched, one of her skis slipped and she shrieked, frantically trying to flatten herself against the slope. A man was peering up at her from a few metres below, shielding his eyes from the sun. Martin recognised Christian.

'Come on!' Christian shouted. 'You've just got to turn.'

'I can't!' Lucy shouted.

'Just turn! Put your skis down the slope and turn!'

Lucy started to cry. She made a whooping noise that travelled in jagged chimes down the valley.

'Come on!' shouted Christian. He lifted his poles and drove them straight down again into the snow. Then he shook his head and looked up into the air. Lucy roared. A moment later she went sliding and shouting down another few metres. Christian didn't watch her. He turned and faced out towards the valley in a posture of contemplation. Martin skied down to Lucy, and as he drew near he saw her face more clearly. Deep grooves of anger striated the skin. Tears and mucus were smeared over her red cheeks. Threads of saliva hung from her mouth. When she saw him she gave a strange grunt, as though she were stranded in an incommunicable unhappiness.

'Follow me down,' he said. 'Just look at my skis and don't look at anything else. Turn where I turn.'

He had no idea whether this would work. He merely desired to unpick her from the snag of what seemed dimly to him to be her femininity. He wanted to comb it out, the whole tangle, until it was straight and clear. He set off slowly. When he looked back he expected not to see her there, but her dark form was looming just behind him. They passed Christian, who seconds later passed them and skied on down to the bottom without stopping. He was waiting for them by the café near the lifts. Lucy took off her skis and waded in her boots through the snow towards him.

'Were you trying to kill me?' she said.

Martin bent down in the sun and undid his skis, pretending not to hear.

'– supposed to be a holiday,' said Lucy, marching past Christian towards the café. They sat down at a table outside in the sun. Martin lit a cigarette and closed his eyes. He

41

would have known where he was just from this, the feeling of the cold sun pressing against his eyelids and the way that every sound and smell had clean edges here, the scent of his coffee and the clear shouts of people coming down the mountain, the light hiss of their skis as they passed. He opened his eyes and there was Lucy, sharp against the blue sky, uncamouflaged, marooned in light.

'I've never been so frightened in my life,' she said garrulously. 'I couldn't understand what I was doing stuck on this cliff of ice with two planks strapped to my feet.'

'That was pretty stupid of me,' said Christian, raking his fingers across his short, light-brown hair. 'It looked easy from the top.'

'I wouldn't make someone I loved go down that slope,' said Lucy.

'I didn't know,' said Christian. 'I couldn't see what it was like further down.'

'Thank God Martin came along,' said Lucy. 'You were so calm, the way you did it. I was absolutely sure I wasn't going to turn and then I just did.'

'You should have lessons,' said Martin. 'By the end of the week you'd be able to go down anything.'

'I know,' said Lucy. 'But this is our first time away since the twins. We really wanted to spend it together.'

The sun was directly in her face and she screwed up her eyes. Sitting there, she looked uncomfortable in her big body. He thought of his daughter and a generalised feeling of pity came over him, for them, for girls, women. When he was growing up, his mother had spoken of men as rigid beings, as part of a whole system of rigidity through which women flowed, like water through a set of pipes. You were made to go this way and that, she implied; you acted not out of your own will, but out of a sense that was half obligation and half compulsion. She spoke about childhood and marriage as though they were the same thing, or a continuation of each other. Sometimes she punished him with his father's borrowed anger, but more often Martin felt incorporated into her submissiveness, her moments of subversion, her long straight stretches of duty. Then, suddenly, she would leave him; she would take her pleasure, without warning. He would enter a room and find that she and his father were embracing, and it was like an embrace of mountains, those two bodies held in a clinch: it seemed catastrophic. Once he had crept out of his bed and come downstairs while his parents were entertaining their friends to dinner, with the idea that he could hook his mother and reel her out of the noisy room. She was deep in conversation with a man on one side of her; she didn't notice Martin, even though he was there. The man said something and his mother laughed so loudly that Martin was startled – she laughed and flung her arms in the air, and it was like the cork exploding from a champagne bottle. He felt that he had seen her as she really was, that everything else he knew of her was a misrepresentation. His parents were divorced now. His father had gone to live with another woman, just as he used to go to the office every day. His mother said she felt free. She said she hadn't felt so good in years. Martin had believed her, until he spent a night at the house one weekend and heard her through the wall crying in her bed. She wailed, like a child, or an animal in pain.

'Is Josephine with the others?' said Lucy.

'I don't know,' said Martin.

'I've never met her before,' said Lucy, over the parapet of her coffee cup. 'She seems nice. I think she was a bit disappointed to be sharing a room with me.' She looked at Martin significantly. 'Don't you think she's pretty?'

'I suppose so,' said Martin.

'If I were Jane,' said Lucy, 'I wouldn't bring my glamorous friends on holiday with me. She's always throwing these women in Thomas's path. I think she does it as a test of his loyalty.'

'You don't know that,' said Christian.

'All I'm saying,' said Lucy, 'is that I wouldn't do it.'

Martin wanted to get back up the mountain. He felt suddenly that he was sliding down a slope of time, in the wrong direction. He wished he hadn't come to this part of the resort; he wished he had stayed on the other side, where he was happy. Thinking this made him realise that happiness was for him an act of subterfuge. The whole flow of his life was towards becoming embroiled. In the hospital, after the baby was born and Dominique had fallen asleep, he had sat holding his daughter in a chair beside the bed and she had looked at him with unfocused, empty eyes; and he had felt in that moment oppressed by her need and by his sense that an onerous job had fallen to him by virtue of his being there awake while her mother slept. His daughter was corresponding with him, assuming that he was the first thing in the world; she was already building herself on his foundations and it was too late to stop her. After that it was he who rose, who walked the silty floor of the night with her while her limitless cries unspooled. Dominique, always tired or in pain or somehow unhappy, always in the end victimised by the things she had created, seemed to exist more and more in a state of unconstrained emotion. The baby got on her nerves – that was the sort of thing she had started to say. It was as if the baby were the culmination of

44

her relationship with concrete things – she was galvanised, by this creature that had come from inside her, to refute every opposition to her feelings. Martin had witnessed the violent expulsion; he had watched Dominique labour with the eerie feeling that he was seeing the agonies not of creation but of rejection. He couldn't, in fact, see how it could be anything else. He hadn't expected birth to be so terrible. It had made him angry, actually angry; with the baby mostly, but also with himself, because it seemed somehow to be his fault. Afterwards he took the baby as he might have taken the evidence of a crime, with the intention of concealing it. He could see now that he had been stupid to act like there was something to apologise for. It gave Dominique the idea that she had been wronged, and this idea was like a door opening in her head, letting out all the other wrongs, everything unfair that had happened to her in her life. A lot of those wrongs were his; he recognised them, surprised, like old keepsakes she'd hoarded that he'd long since thought lost. It had seemed to him that his absence had become necessary. It would be like a fast, after gorging on emotion. He hoped that it would be the glue that would stick the two of them, Dominique and the baby, back together.

He left Lucy and Christian sitting on the terrace in the sun and took the lift back up to the top of the mountain. The sky was a hard, enamelled blue and the pistes were busy. He looked at the other people; he watched the way they skied, seeing them in little frames against the white snow, as though in those few seconds he was lifting them out of their lives, each one. Comprehension unfurled from his brain in every direction into the empty air. He felt his mind meeting other minds, one wordless encounter after another. He forgot, almost, that he possessed the power of speech: the speed, the downwards motion, the frictionless surface of snow pressed on the creases of his consciousness like a methodical iron. Late in the afternoon he met Josephine. He was standing in the queue for the lift and she barged in behind him, saying his name and gripping his arm. He had forgotten about her completely – he couldn't remember who she was, although she came at him in such detail in the clear mountain light that she seemed almost unbearably real. He could see every strand of her hair, every pore. Her voice addressing him was excruciating. All his senses felt tender and for a moment it was too much, the welter of association, it was like a thousand tiny hammers hitting him.

'I just saw a pile-up,' she said, sitting next to him on the lift. 'Three of them, all coming from different directions. Splat.' She clapped her gloved hands together. 'One of them flew about ten feet up in the air. I thought he was dead for sure. I went over to have a look and he was just lying there staring at the sky with this really weird expression on his face.'

'Shock,' said Martin.

'I suppose so,' said Josephine. 'They took him away on a stretcher.'

They sat in silence on the swaying lift. The cables reached upwards like a great necklace to the top of the mountain. The sun had moved behind a ridge and the afternoon light was ebbing. A blade of cold was spreading palely across the valley. It was almost time to go down.

'This is it for me,' said Josephine. She threw back her head and closed her eyes. 'Then it's back to another evening of married bliss.'

The sarcastic way she spoke annoyed him. He had met

girls like Josephine before – hundreds of them, it seemed. They never did anything real; they never knew anything, they just sat there like a bored audience, whispering in each other's ears.

'What's wrong with marriage?' he said.

She turned to him with a look of mock-incredulity.

'*Nothing*,' she said. 'It's just not the world's most thrilling spectator sport.'

'It isn't supposed to be,' said Martin.

'I nearly got married,' said Josephine presently. 'I had an engagement ring and everything. I gave it back,' she added, 'in case you were wondering.'

The humming cables shrieked faintly overhead and then ground to a halt. The chairs swayed silently in the air.

'It was sort of symbolic,' she said.

'Of what?'

'Of – I don't know, of a *transaction*,' said Josephine, gesturing with her gloved hands. 'It was like someone had slapped a sticker on me saying "sold". Personally,' she said, 'I couldn't take it. I had to liberate myself from a whole way of thinking. A whole mind-set.'

'What sort of mind-set?' said Martin.

'Well,' sighed Josephine, 'I suppose I thought that if someone wanted me it meant that I was worth something. I suffer from a fear of rejection. But also I wanted to get through it, to get to the end. Like the end of a story. It was me that pushed him into it. He was quite happy as we were. I think he felt like he'd been run over.'

'Poor bloke,' said Martin.

'Oh, it wasn't so bad,' said Josephine. 'It was an experience. Anyway, I'm not the only one. Loads of women are like that. It's our mothers' fault. They flog us through

47

school and university and then treat us like failures because we haven't settled down and had kids.'

The cables juddered into motion again and the chair sailed forwards through the cold, still air.

'Babies, you know, that's different,' said Josephine. 'That would have been a completely different thing. I've got this friend, his wife has left him on his own with two children. I would *never* do that.'

They got out at the top just as the lift closed. People were pouring down the mountain ahead of the blue light of evening. Far below, the lights had come on in the little town.

'Do you want to go down together?' said Martin. 'You don't want to get lost at the end of the day.'

'Whatever,' said Josephine.

He kept behind her all the way down. She was a good skier; she picked out a more difficult route than he would have chosen. After a while he forgot everything again; he just watched her darting ahead of him through the trees and let his skis chase after her small, dark form. Near the bottom she went over a ridge and whooped as she flew into the air, flinging her poles above her head. He went after her, without making a sound.

In the evening they went to a hot little restaurant up a side-street that served dense, oleaginous plates of potato and sausage and cheese. It rocked like the hull of a ship with the loud voices and ruddy faces of skiers. Jane and Thomas talked of their day, in which they had travelled by bus to a different part of the resort to ski. Martin had been vaguely looking out for them on the mountain; he had expected to spend some time skiing with Thomas, but increasingly he had the feeling that Jane was keeping Thomas away from his old life, as though he were an addict and Martin a source of temptation. Jane annoyed Martin. Chewing his food he felt as though his mouth were full of her. She looked at him sharply, head cocked, sensing his distaste.

'How's Dominique doing?' she said.

'Fine, I think.'

'Has she started expressing her milk?'

Martin was seized by the desire to slap her, to exhort her violently to think about something else. Jane and Thomas talked constantly about the right time for having a baby. It was two years away, or perhaps three, Martin couldn't remember. They didn't think you could just have one. They were ironing out their lives in preparation, starching and folding and putting away their youth, their excitement, their spontaneity. Jane had visited Dominique in hospital. Dominique said she felt like a delinquent teenager being interviewed by a social worker.

'No,' he said. 'Not yet.'

'I never managed to do that,' said Lucy. 'I got one of those machines, but I hated it. I felt like a cow being milked.'

'Please,' said Josephine, placing her hand on her stomach. 'I'm eating.'

'It's perfectly natural, you know,' said Lucy. Her face was red. 'There's nothing wrong with it.'

'Well, at least take pity on this poor guy, then,' said Josephine, clapping a hand lightly on Martin's arm. 'He's come all the way to Switzerland to get away from that stuff.'

The two other women stared at Martin. Josephine's hand was small and manicured and she wore several rings. Dominique wore no jewellery; her hands were large and angular and sparsely fleshed. He found Dominique's hands

49

mesmerising. They seemed to assert something about her, a moral quality: her hands were true; they were incorruptible.

'I must say,' said Lucy presently, 'Dominique is a lot more relaxed than I ever was at that stage. I wouldn't let Christian out of my sight.'

'In a way, though,' said Jane, 'there's not that much for fathers to do early on. At the beginning the bond's with the mother. The father's role comes later.'

'What difference does it make?' said Josephine. 'They'll hate you both in the end.'

'That's exactly the kind of thing my sister would say,' said Lucy sourly.

'I must meet her,' said Josephine.

'Only someone who didn't have children could say that sort of thing,' continued Lucy.

'We've decided that Tom isn't going to take his paternity leave straight away,' said Jane. 'He's going to take it later, when I'm back at work. That way he'll be able to have full responsibility.'

'What a thought,' said Josephine.

'I'm timing it to coincide with the World Cup,' said Thomas.

'You're not actually pregnant, are you?' said Lucy, in a low voice.

'God no,' said Jane. 'I've got to do at least a year at Browning's before I qualify.'

'For what?' said Josephine. 'A pregnancy test?'

'Maternity leave,' said Jane.

'Wow,' said Josephine, spearing a sausage with her fork. 'Let's hope alien life-forms from outer space don't invade the planet before then.'

Martin stopped at the phone booth on the way home.

Dominique's mother answered. Dominique was asleep. The baby was fine, she was right there on her lap. Martin asked her if she was getting any sleep and she said not much. I've got the rest of my life to sleep, she said. She's a party animal, your daughter. He guessed from that that Dominique still wasn't getting up to feed her. A stone of worry lodged itself in his chest. Dominique had become distraught almost straight away about being woken at night. She would lie on her back in the dark and cry while the baby cried in her cot next to their bed. Martin always got up quickly now and got the baby out of the room before she could wake Dominique up. Sometimes they fell asleep together on the sofa. He gave her bottles of formula milk that he mixed and stood in a row before he went to bed. The midwife had said Dominique would never establish breastfeeding that way, but he didn't see what else he could do. When he got back to the apartment the others were asleep.

They had two more days of good weather and then clouds closed in around the mountain, swaddling the pistes and lifts in fog. Martin hung around the little town alone while the others went ice skating. He had become, somehow, detached from the group. Lucy and Christian had joined forces with Jane and Thomas, travelling about on buses together to distant pistes and even spending one afternoon when the weather was good sightseeing in the local town. Thomas was a good skier; Martin didn't know how he could stand it, the confinement, the wasted time. Staring through gift-shop windows, Martin felt his presence on the holiday begin to seem more and more brutal. All around him people were giving in to each other, denying themselves. He and Dominique had made an agreement that they weren't going to be like that. It was a sort of contract, because she wanted a baby and he didn't, not yet anyway – and she had promised that her obsession, the sharp point of her determination would pass through him quickly and painlessly, leaving him unharmed. He should have known better, but he hadn't. He had thought that she possessed some secret knowledge, that a mysterious fund of femininity lay beneath her like a pale root. He had thought that she became something else when she ceased to be visible to him. Instead she had spread herself like frantic ivy over every available surface; she had covered him in needy tendrils; he could tear them off but they just grew back. He had finally spoken to her on the phone – she said breastfeeding hadn't worked out so she had abandoned it. He was silently aggrieved that she had just stopped without asking him. He felt conspired against in his absence. He felt too that he had failed to protect his daughter. It had been gestating in him, this feeling, and now his hours of inactivity had brought it to life. As a child, he had been for a period fixated by the realisation that he was bound to existence by a series of tethers. His shadow, his heartbeat, the ceaseless work of breathing had all, for a while, fascinated and oppressed him. Sometimes he tried not to breathe. Sometimes he would climb a wall or a tree to see if his shadow followed him. He had in his mind a narrow, high place where he would be sufficient to himself.

By afternoon the lifts were open and he went up. People had given up on the day and the mountain was more or less empty. He skied under the ropes at the edge of the piste and headed off into wilderness. This was what he liked best, skiing in the trees. Today he skied dangerously, wildly dodging rocks, hurtling down unmarked valleys. It was still cloudy and he could see only a few feet in front of him. He felt a vicious carelessness of himself. He revelled in his skill and in his right to expend himself. He wound down a long, tree-studded slope and came out fast the other end, going over the next incline without stopping. It was bare and very steep; at the bottom he could see the village lights. He turned his skis straight down the hill, wondering if he could make the village in one run. He was going so fast that he nearly closed his eyes, like someone falling asleep at the wheel of the car. Just then his skis abruptly levelled out, and by the time he realised he had hit a path he had nearly crossed it. He skidded sideways but the momentum of the hill threw him over the path and into empty space on the other side. He didn't know what had happened. There was a thick crust of snow overhanging the sheer drop below the path and somehow he was splayed on it, clinging, with nothing beneath him. Someone was speaking to him in French. A ski pole nosed against his face and he grabbed it and felt himself dragged back on to the path. He had lost his skis. When he stood up he fell over straight away. The man helped him up. It was a ski monitor. He was shaking his head and shouting. Martin couldn't speak. The man began to talk in English. You are very lucky, he said. I follow you, you are very lucky. Martin said that he was sorry. Mad, said the man, *fou*. He offered to walk with Martin back to the village but Martin waved him on. The mountain was turning blue as dusk fell. His legs twitched violently as he walked slowly down the path towards the village. It was dark by the time he got back to the apartment. The others were out. He got into bed and lay curled on his side.

The next day was the last. Martin rented new skis and went up with Christian. Lucy didn't want to ski; she said she was going to stay down and pack and shop for presents for the twins.

'Oh, come on,' said Martin. 'It's your last day.'

Christian stood by the apartment door in his jacket and goggles. He didn't say anything.

'No, really,' said Lucy. 'I think it would be tempting fate. I've got this far without breaking anything. It'd be just my luck.'

Martin saw that she hadn't enjoyed the holiday. She was desperate to go home. There was plenty of time to pack in the evening, but she wanted to do it now, as though to hasten their departure.

'To be honest,' said Christian, as they walked down the road towards the lifts, 'I don't mind having a day on my own. It's quite tiring, being with someone who can't do it. The ground we've covered this week, it would have been quicker to walk.'

'You should have said,' said Martin. 'I would have skied with her a couple of afternoons.'

'She should have taken classes,' said Christian.

'Maybe next time,' said Martin.

'I don't think either of us has got much out of it. It's pretty stupid, when you think how much it's cost. And we didn't even get to share a room. Our first time away since the children, and we didn't get to share a room.'

'I don't quite know how that happened,' said Martin.

'Lucy didn't want to,' said Christian bitterly. 'That's what happened. She runs a mile every time I lay a hand on her.'

'It was a bad arrangement,' said Martin.

'I didn't realise,' said Christian, 'that once we'd had the twins that would be it. I mean, I love them and everything, but sometimes I think, God, whatever happened to our life? Was that it? Two years of going out for the odd curry – and half that time we spent talking about whether we were going to have children and when, and what we were going to call them. I wish now,' said Christian, slumping next to Martin on the lift, 'that I'd done more when I had the chance.'

The top of the mountain, its steep faces, its spikes, stood embedded in Martin's heart like a claw. It was strange, but the previous day's accident had made him want it even more, to be alone with it. The soles of his feet pricked with anticipation. He said goodbye to Christian, vaguely promising to see him somewhere at the bottom, and flew away into the white air. He skied some difficult runs – he had never skied so well, so unconsciously – but by lunchtime the fact of his return was with him. It was like a wall in front of him. The reality of Dominique and the baby was beginning to show through the veil of his absence, coming in glaring flashes as if through rents in his dreams. He tried to set the afternoon afloat, but the thought of what awaited him brought him down from the mountain early. He packed his things back at the apartment and lay on his bed reading a book. After a while he must have fallen asleep, a grey, light sleep from which he was woken by Thomas throwing a towel at his head.

'What time is it?' said Martin, sitting up.

'Show time,' said Thomas.

Josephine was standing behind him in her skiing clothes. Her eyes were dark, mischievous slits. She was giggling.

'This is going to be so tacky,' she said. She drew forwards and placed her hand on Thomas's shoulder. They gazed down at Martin where he sat on the bed. 'Come on, dad,' she said. 'Move those bones.'

'Where are we going?'

'Up ze hill,' said Thomas. 'In ze dark.'

The others had gone to see a film. Thomas and Josephine

had just missed them, they said. Martin saw that they had done it on purpose and could hardly be bothered to lie about it. The resort was staging an event called 'Skiing by Moonlight'. They had opened the lifts and floodlit one of the pistes, and were playing piped music through loudspeakers at the top of the mountain. Martin unpacked his skiing clothes. The three of them walked along the slushy, faintly lit road. Martin had a feeling of alarm, as though he were a passenger in a car that was moving steadily away from his destination. He had prepared himself to go home, and now he was back outside again with his skis in his hand and his whole body summoning itself at the prospect of ascent. It should have made no difference, but it did – in his chest there was the feeling of a gash opening, a scar that he saw would never mend, because no matter how carefully he stitched it up it lay across a part of himself whose motion was fundamental. Now that the baby had come his life would be lived against a mounting force of limitation.

He watched as Thomas grabbed a handful of snow and crept up behind Josephine to stuff it down the back of her jacket. She cried out, and for a moment she seemed lit up as though by electricity – Martin saw life flowing through her, and it struck him how selfishly it sought its course, this river of sensation, how vain and yet how irresistible was the desire to restrain it. To do what you wanted, when there were so many other things to be done, when all the beauty lay in going back and not forwards – it was a sort of wisdom that his daughter had already taught him, that his wants were a kind of delusion, an overgrowth, like the tired, laden branches of a neglected garden. The pain of cutting back, in order to begin again: he had felt it many times already in her short life, had seen that by this work he would save himself, and yet it was hard; because in spite of the fact her small body refunded to him some of his own lost innocence, he remained adult; he retained a tendency towards freedom. Dominique's unhappiness suggested to him that she had never been free in the first place. The baby had displaced her, as though in the queue for the world's attention. She hadn't yet got what she wanted. The thought of how she would get it frightened him.

They reached the lifts and somehow Josephine and Thomas were separated as the chairs came round the carousel. Josephine was carried upwards into the darkness alone, while Martin and Thomas squashed into a chair together. Martin caught a foolish look on Thomas's handsome face, of surprise and disappointment. Ahead of them he could make out Josephine's still, silent form as it hung suspended in the freezing dark. Tomorrow Jane and Thomas would return to their London flat and Josephine would fall away from them, like a clod of earth flung from a turning wheel.

'This is good,' said Thomas, jiggling slightly in his seat.

'Yeah.'

'You must want to get home,' Thomas suddenly added.

'Sort of,' said Martin flatly. 'It's been strange being away. I had the feeling that I might just forget to go back.'

He told Thomas a bit about Dominique and the problems with the baby, and to his surprise Thomas was unstoppered and his essence, what he used to be and what Martin realised he must be still, flowed out. Martin talked on, and Thomas began to seem more and more to him like a point of contact both earthly and divine, a robed father to whom Martin, the vagrant, the unquiet soul, had returned to seek counsel. They rose together weightlessly towards the crest of the mountain. The touch of life had never been so light. He barely felt it – it was as though gravity had freed the things he knew.

'It's a kind of arrogance,' he said, 'to think that you can choose what happens to you.'

'I thought that,' said Thomas. 'I thought it was better to do nothing. But now I want to do everything.'

'What's everything?'

'Jane's not going to be around so much when we get back,' said Thomas. 'She's got to do macho hours at this new job. And travelling, a week or so out of each month. I think it's good. I think it's a good thing.'

'Why?'

'All this time you spend together,' said Thomas, 'and at the end you haven't made anything of it.' He fiddled with the straps of his poles. 'So now we want money. And we want to have a good time.'

They got off the lifts. Hardly anyone else was there. They looked around for Josephine but she had already gone. The sound of piano music, frayed with static, ebbed through the loudspeakers. Floodlights had been placed in the snow, forming a yellow river that meandered out of sight. The mountain looked ethereal with the prohibition of its darkness lifted. Martin felt himself connected to a series of moments in his life, which seemed to disclose themselves deeper and deeper in him, one after the other, like a chain of lights. Thomas set off ahead of him, hooting and waving his arm as he snaked down the ghostly piste. Martin watched him until he disappeared. The sky was a dome of stars. He would never be here again. He hesitated like a diver over the still surface of water, and launched himself.

The Sacrifices

In the summer of 20– I went back to the old house. It was a
day of uninteresting weather, the kind of grey, motionless
day that occurs with countless frequency in that part of the
country. I had not been to the house, nor to that part of the
country, for twenty years and yet I had the impression that
for all that time it had sat as though in a trance beneath a
low, stultified sky that was indistinguishable from the sky
under which we had packed our things and left the house
for the last time. I parked my car at the bottom of the rutted
lane and walked the rest of the way. I didn't know who lived
in the house now. As I walked along I caught glimpses
of the lower part of the garden, whose boundary ran down
the lane on the other side of a bramble hedge. The hedge
was wild and overgrown and the garden appeared and
receded several times through its branches. There was no
wind at all. Everything stood gelid and silent in the flat grey
light. I reached the gate and saw the drive, which looked
much smaller than I remembered but otherwise identical,
as though over time it had expanded like a living thing in
my memory. At the end of the drive stood the house.
A shiny car was parked outside it, but apart from that it
looked deserted. It stared straight ahead with the passive
expression of a horse in harness.

The house was quite handsome, masculine rather than

graceful, with a square front and a square porch attached to it. It was surrounded by tall trees and beyond that by the garden, which rolled away out of sight. As I child I spent a lot of time in the garden, which had many different parts that sounded together like the different instruments in an orchestra and made a great noise that only I could hear. I walked up the path that was the continuation of the lane and looked over the fence. At first sight I had thought the house to be neglected, but now I could see that this was not so. A chicken coop had been built beside the old barn and the birds pecked quietly inside it. Vegetables were being grown in neat rows and a new greenhouse had been put in: through the glass I could see stacks of little pots and obedient lines of seedlings, and a pair of gardening gloves hanging with a hat from a peg. There was no one about, and after a while this fact struck me as being in some way sinister. I wished that I was not alone, not because I was frightened but because the accomplishment of the tidy vegetables and the pecking birds, the strange shiny car and the windless silence seemed to be robbing me of the sense of my own identity. As a child, I had a private distrust of the stability of everyday things. It always seemed possible to me that I would wake up one day to find that what was familiar to me had undergone a malevolent process of transformation. This is what appeared in that moment to have happened to the house. My house, the real house, had been mysteriously annihilated and replaced by this deceptively smiling simulacrum. I had come alone, not because I wanted to, but because visiting the house had seemed like a good thing to do with all the time I now had on my hands. I would never have thought of it had I been busy. But also, as the years have passed I have become increasingly aware of a certain magnetism somewhere in my past. I am more and more drawn to the contemplation of things that happened a long time ago, things which, like certain paintings, seem to gain in clarity the further away from them I stand. When I try to locate the source of this magnetism it is always the house that I see. I don't know why my mind has chosen to fix itself on something so concrete. It is the same with people you once cared about. When you meet them again you see your feelings still imprisoned in them, unavailing, like jewels locked in a casket.

After a while I went back down the lane towards the village. Fulford isn't much of a village. There's just a little shop that sells packets and tins and sweets in jars, and a modern redbrick pub that stands darkly in a pool of tarmac at the crossroads. It is surrounded by flat fields where the roads run perfectly straight to the horizon. There are one or two grand houses that sit back behind a veil of trees, but most of the housing is new. It stands in clusters in the stubbly arable prairie, as though in shyness or hesitation, built around fresh, black cul-de-sac roads that are all curved, in spite of the fact that every other road in the place is straight. In the mornings we used to wait at the crossroads for the school bus and the road was so flat and straight that we could see the bus coming from a mile or more away, small and furious as a beetle as it ploughed along the grey furrow.

In winter the wet, dark-green land ruminated in the damp grey light that came from a sky always wadded with cloud, but in summer a dry, floury haze would come in off the fields of wheat and corn so that everything was almost colourless and the sun was held in a beautiful gauze in the air. Long, warm winds would sometimes ruffle the yellow and brown pelt of the harvest and make the heavy trees rustle. The flatness was oceanic. If you lay on your back and closed your eyes you could feel a slow motion like the motion of waves.

I lived in the square house up the potholed lane with my parents and my twin sister, Lucy, and they loomed large in the flat landscape, which was so empty of obvious entertainment and where time passed slowly, laboriously, as though each hour were being manufactured by hand. Lucy is eight minutes older than me, a distinction she cultivated in those days by spending most of her time either sequestered in her room or with our mother in the kitchen, making things. They made biscuits and patchwork quilts, collages, peppermint creams, corn dollies and lavender bags. They painted fir-cones and arranged flowers and they talked, conversations that passed over me in wordless cadences, like music. I didn't listen to what they said, just to the sound they made saying it. I watched the house fill piece by piece with shadow, until its rooms and corridors seemed to stand at the inky bottom of a well and my mother switched on the lights.

In those days, my parents had a couple who worked for them, a husband and wife called Jim and Sally. They lived in the village in a small redbrick house that stood on the road just beyond the furthest boundary of our garden. There was a gate down there, and two or three times a week Jim and Sally would come through it and walk up the lawn to the house. Sally cleaned while Jim looked after the garden; they were a servile version of my parents, a practical-minded counterfeit. Sally was small and tough and tanned, with a little head like a walnut. She told me terrible stories about people she knew, while her bare muscled arms castigated the bathtub with a sponge and bleach. A friend of hers had been electrocuted in the bath, apparently. She had been lying there drying her hair and had dropped the hairdryer into the water. It could happen with anything, Sally said, a radio, a toaster, anything electric. I remarked that it would be a good way to kill somebody and Sally agreed.

One afternoon I was looking out of my bedroom window at the back garden, where Jim was digging a flowerbed, and I saw him fall abruptly over on to his side. He fell so quickly that it was almost as though he had thrown himself to the earth out of some mysterious compulsion. He lay there, curled and motionless. His big body looked soft and limp, like the body of the rabbit our cat had recently laid reverently on the doorstep. I ran to tell my mother and Jim was taken to hospital. It transpired that he had had an attack of vertigo. It's all in your ear, Sally said. Your ear gets out of kilter and the world turns upside down. She said that Jim was now at home, pinned to the bed in terror. The world was still upside down and they didn't know when or how it was going to turn the right way up. I went to see him, partly to take some flowers from the garden that my mother had picked and partly to see whether, in Jim's room, the world really was upside down. I imagined him in bed on the ceiling, clutching his sheets in fright. I did not expect to feel, entering Sally and Jim's house for the first time, a sense of shame and embarrassment at how little I had considered the fact of their marriage and life together; and how modest was the extent of this fact as represented by the small brown rooms in which they lived. Sally took the flowers and gave me a biscuit from a tin. Jim wasn't up to visitors, she said. I heard him moaning upstairs, hoarse, preternatural, wordless sounds that made the house shake.

Boredom, like a geological force, gradually sculpted my sister and me into different shapes. Lucy, with her interests and her handicrafts, her conversations with my mother and her urgent business in her bedroom, was more sheltered than I from the slow rain of time. Lucy's bedroom was full of the evidence of her industry. She had collections of everything, shells, stamps, dolls, little china figurines, all of whose positions on the shelves she marked with military precision so as to foil attempts at intrusion. My own room was full of underwater light which I used to watch swimming around the walls and getting caught in the shadow of the tree outside the window, whose forked fingers projected themselves in like reeds. I didn't do much there: I just lay on my bed listening to the sounds people made in other rooms and trying to work out from these sounds what they were doing and what time of day it was. I sometimes pretended that I was deaf, or blind, or asleep. I tried to imagine what it was like to be dead.

I liked having nothing to do, but my formlessness constantly brought me to the boundaries of my parents' authority. Like a cow in a field, I would roam aimlessly until the prick of the electric fence rebuked me. A minute later I would forget again that it was there. I once spoke to my husband, Robert, about the atmosphere of disapproval that attended my every action as a child, and about how I was deceived by its dormancy; how I would unexpectedly animate it, like a hand animates a glove. I thought it might cast some light on the difficulties we were having, but Robert did not seem to find it particularly significant. He didn't give much credence to the idea that experiences in childhood leave indelible marks on your life, except, as he put it, in cases of exceptional trauma. Robert is a hospital consultant; his medical training has given him an unsentimental view of things. But visiting the old house, it struck me all the same as strange that Robert had never seen the place where I had grown up. It gave substance to the feeling I had had for some time, that I was sent away from that house in order to live my life among strangers.

In those days I spent a lot of time riding around on my bike, and sometimes I would set off along one of the straight roads to see how far I could go. I did not believe that those roads could just go on and on like that without reaching some meaningful conclusion. I sensed that if I followed one for long enough, until I had disobeyed every last injunction in myself to turn back, something would happen. And indeed I did once succeed in penetrating the membrane that seemed to lie at the limits of my experience. I cycled for so long that I got lost. I reached one junction in the road and then another, and all at once I was in a strange place, with houses I didn't recognise. It was a village like Fulford, perhaps slightly smaller. It was marooned in the same flat fields. I felt a desolate certainty that somehow I had reached a place that was further-flung even than the place where I lived. I laid down my bike and stood forlornly outside the telephone box, hoping to remember my number, for I was suddenly very frightened: not only because I was lost but also because trouble had laid its hand on my shoulder in that empty village, and I could feel my parents' anger, like a distant earthquake whose tremors were rolling steadily out across the flat land towards me. I began to cry, not separate tears but sheets of water that flooded painlessly down my face. At that moment a man came out of one of the houses. He was a black man, not old, although his frizzy hair was grey. He was wearing flip-flops and a striped shirt with no collar. He asked me if I was lost and where I lived. I told him the name of the village and he said he would take me home. He went back inside and came out with a pair of shoes on. Then he took some round wire-framed glasses out of the pocket of his shirt and placed them carefully on his face. He had some difficulty getting my bike into the back of his car, which was a beige hatchback that leaned over to one side. I watched him, embarrassed, as he manoeuvred it this way and that. He went slowly back into the house and came out again with a ball of string, which he used to tie down the door over the protruding back wheel. All this took a very long time and I was becoming more and more anxious. Finally he yanked open the passenger door and I sat down on the springy seat. Don't worry, he said as we chuntered along, they'll be very happy to see you. I wanted to believe him; I wondered whether, as an adult, he might even have some say in the matter, but when we came up the drive my mother came out of the house and her face was cleaved by anger. She and Dr Lakey, as I discovered he was called, conversed there on the drive, my mother stiff with politeness and Dr Lakey shaking his head and saying 'Oh well' in a sing-song voice and laughing ever louder as my mother became more curt. As he left he put his arm around my shoulders and gave me a fierce little hug, and his skin was so hot and dry in the damp garden that I felt an urge to defect to him, to be carried away from the gloom of my mother's anger; but he got back into his little car and went away, and I was smacked and sent to my room. Shortly afterwards I heard my mother and a friend of hers talking about Dr Lakey in the kitchen. He was a GP in the local town, apparently. The friend said she could never have him as her doctor. She said she couldn't bear the thought of his hands touching her.

At night I lay in my bed and my mind projected itself like a cone of light into the country darkness, growing wider and wider until the darkness swallowed it. Often I couldn't sleep, and sometimes I would get up and go along the hall to my parents' room. I would stand beside their bed, wanting to wake them but not daring to. I thought that if I stood there for long enough they might wake anyway. In sleep their faces were stern and stony. On the plinth of the bed their bodies were vast, impassive. I imagined myself perching there, like a bird on a monument. It would begin to seem terrible, the idea of them melting, waking, and so after a while I would leave the room more quietly than I had entered it and I would go back to bed.

I have watched Robert sleep, too. He sleeps like something discarded in a hurry and flung on the floor. You can look at him at any time of night and he will always be in the same position as that in which he fell.

In the mornings Lucy and I took the bus to school in the nearby town, and after school I would sometimes go and visit my friend Roxanne, who lived on the other side of the village in an uproarious realm of swirl-patterned carpets and barking dogs. Roxanne should have been at school too, but she frequently wasn't. She stayed up late and then missed the bus in the morning because she was still asleep. I never met Roxanne's mother. I don't know what happened to her. But Roxanne had an older sister called Stacy who was supposed to look after her. Stacy was small and squat with a flat round face and a mouth that curled at the corners. She did her eyes so that they curled at the corners too. Stacy was always to be found in her room, where lacy underwear spilled out of drawers and every surface was covered with mascara wands and jars of nail polish and the special combs she used to make her hair stand out in a frizzy cloud. Roxanne and I would sit on Stacy's unmade bed while she teased her hair expertly and told us stories that gave me bad dreams, about murders and mutilations and the strange, ironic ways in which you could be unlucky. Stacy wore knee-high boots that zipped up the side. She had to put them on before she got out of bed in the morning. Once you stood up, she said, all the blood ran down to your legs and made them fat. She had to lie down to put her jeans on too. Sometimes Roxanne and I had to help her, Roxanne holding the two sides together over Stacy's thick white abdomen while I tried to drive the zip up its furrow. One day the zip refused to go any further. We kneaded Stacy's stomach and sat on her, to no avail. Stacy announced her intention of refusing all food and drink until she could do her jeans up again. A few weeks later Roxanne told me that Stacy was pregnant. I worried that when the baby came out it would be squashed from that occasion on which we had tried to flatten Stacy's stomach. The memory of her solid, resisting flesh haunted me. I felt that we ought to tell someone what we had done. For her eleventh birthday, Roxanne's father bought her a case of Babycham and a pair of red satin knickers. Whenever I returned from Roxanne's house my parents would darkly confer, like an audience that is not enjoying the play, but all the same I told them about Roxanne's birthday presents. And, accordingly, they forbade me from going to Roxanne's house any more, so that as I had hoped I was removed from the scene of the crime. Secretly I still worried about the deformed baby, but as it turned out I never saw Stacy again.

When we returned from school my sister Lucy would go to her room and close the door. Like a novice she waited there, as though for a revelation. She was privy to my parents' views about the world and so she knew this revelation would come: she knew that the life in the village was a prelude, and that the real life had yet to begin. She waited in her room for a new development. I have the impression that I was never told we were being sent away to boarding school, just as I have the impression that Lucy always knew. Rather, the knowledge came slowly over me, like a change of season. In a department store in the nearest city my mother bought my sister and me new uniforms, purchasing each item in consultation with a detailed list. I understood that the old order had decayed and was being swept away, in spite of the fact that my experience of it was incomplete. It was as though my plate had been removed from the table with half the food untasted. I felt that I had failed to secure the definitive territories of my family existence. I was not certain, in other words, that my parents loved me: it seemed possible that had I behaved differently they might not be sending me away. I sensed that I was being removed because they disapproved of me, yet I couldn't see where my chance had been, nor what I would have done with it had I even recognised it. Those long hours in the flat village and the damp green garden, in the house outside whose windows the world appeared to be sleeping, had been lived with no particular expectation, except that they would continue. Now I was seized by the yearning to go back and live them again in order to find out why they had ended.

My new school was in a convent, so I was surrounded by nuns. Their potato-plain faces against the black of their habits were like faces spotlit on a stage, sadly soliloquising.

They sometimes spoke of the life they'd given up, the life of marriage and children, as though it were an overcrowded tourist attraction they'd sensibly decided to forgo on their travels. The nuns retained a quality of stubbornness that the other adults I knew did not possess. I have often found children to possess this same quality. It is as though a steel rod runs through them, which only certain experiences in life have the power to break. For a period, as a child, I had wanted to be a nun, but it was not that kind of nun I had in mind. In the school chapel, where we went to Mass in the early mornings, there were statues of women – saints and the Virgin Mary – whose stone forms I used to watch emerging from the darkness as the sun rose and distilled its pale light through the chapel windows. Their mute, tender faces, glimpsed as though still in their prison of night, filled me with feelings of comfort.

I was rarely alone at school: I slept and ate and sat in classrooms alongside other girls. The pressure of constant association was so great that I felt as though I was living underwater. In the evenings the other girls would lie around the dormitory in their underwear, in groups like bored, basking seals. They would paint their toenails from small vials of blood-red lacquer. They would conduct inexpert conversations that tended inevitably towards cruelty. A subject would enter their midst, like a forest creature stepping into a clearing, and they would surround it, at first playful, then taunting, until with increasing savagery they would bring it down among them. I wanted to go home. I would think of my parents' house with its empty bedrooms and a feeling of opportunity would come over me; a feeling that the time when we lived together lay not behind me but in the future. I forgot that it was they who had sent my sister and me away. Instead, my memory of my family occurred to me as a brilliant idea that somehow, when I saw my parents, I could never remember to tell them about, even though I was sure they would agree that it would solve everything.

I don't know what my mother did all day, with my father out at work and my sister and me away. I think now of those hours she hoarded and I feel as though I have been robbed of an inheritance. If only I could have seen how she spent them, perhaps I could have forgotten them; but instead I retain the suspicion that she has them still, somewhere about her person – that, though hidden, those hours still exist. I see now that it was never expected that I would live the same kind of life that she had lived. My parents assumed that I would pass exams and go to university. My mother tried, without much sincerity, to give the impression that she had been denied opportunities of which I was fortunate to be availed, but actually I think she regarded herself as lucky. In her own eyes, with her husband and children and house in the country, she was a success. For a brief period, after I had started university and felt life beginning to pass through me like a shrilling, calling carnival, I pitied her her limited existence; but in the years that followed that pity turned slowly, grindingly on its axis, until finally it returned to her her lost authority; until it was she who pitied me.

Robert has a son called Joseph. Joseph lives with his mother, Samantha. Robert met Samantha when he was in medical school. She was working in a bar and one evening Robert went there. He has always been unduly ashamed of the way in which, on a Friday night, he and his medical-student friends would swiftly and determinedly drink themselves into a stupor in order to relieve their exhaustion and anxiety. Robert has a great sense of his own dignity. It was on one of these evenings that he found himself in Samantha's bar, and with the same swiftness and determination that he drank he went home with her and spent the night. It was the only night they spent together, so he has told me. The next morning he was hardly able to recall what had happened. Some weeks later Samantha contacted him via his college and told him that she was pregnant.

There was never any question of them living together. They hardly knew each other, and besides, Samantha didn't want to. What she wanted was for Robert to pay for the maintenance of their child, and in exchange to see Joseph at weekends if he chose. Samantha was twenty-five, Robert a year older. He regarded this sequence of events as entirely catastrophic, a view that hardly altered in the years that followed, even though he loved Joseph and saw him regularly. I could never quite bring myself to ask him why he found it so terrible. It always seemed to relate to those long-ago nights of drinking – which, incidentally, were never from that day repeated – and to the loss of control they brought with them. It was as though some stalking enemy had, in that unguarded moment, been given its dark opportunity.

In spite of their businesslike arrangement, after Joseph was born Samantha immediately began to make demands of Robert. She would call him night and day, crying, saying that if he didn't come round she didn't know what she would do. He would often arrive to find the baby imprisoned in his cot, screaming, while Samantha lay on the sofa in the next-door room reading magazines or watching television. Samantha left Joseph with other people, some of whom she hardly knew. Once she left him with a neighbour, and when she came back the woman had gone, taking the baby with her. The woman didn't return until late in the evening, by which time Robert had called the police. For a long time Robert was tormented by anxiety and by feelings of insecurity when he was away from Joseph, and yet his existence was, as far as Robert was concerned, so unpremeditated that he found it impossible to broach these issues with Samantha. Once, when Joseph was a toddler, she took him to the park and a dog attacked him. Samantha ran away. She told Robert afterwards that she went to get help, which I suppose makes a sort of sense, but even now I find the image of her running hard to get out of my mind. Joseph had teethmarks on his side and leg that never healed. When he was younger and I sometimes used to see him naked, the sight of those marks would take my breath away. He was always frightened of dogs. It used to drive his father mad, the way he wouldn't go ten yards from the house or the car on his own in case he met one. What was strange was that when Joseph was ten or so Samantha got a dog herself. It was a little yappy white thing, not at all fierce, but even so. Joseph pretended that he liked that dog. He used to let it lick his face, where livid bumps of acne were beginning to break through the skin.

At the time Joseph was born I was living with a man I didn't love. I found a strange satisfaction in this arrangement, although I always had to remind myself of what it was, when he embraced me or said that he loved me, that I enjoyed about the blankness I felt in return. Then I would remember my mother's cold, sleeping face, and the day that I was sent away from our house, and a feeling of rightness and relief would come over me. Sometimes I felt as though not to love might become my life's occupation, so appropriate were its sensations and yet so inconclusive. No matter how often I fed it, my urge to deny love would always return.

My lover was born with a hole in his heart. When he was eighteen months old they operated on it. I suppose they just sewed it up. There was no scar or mark on his skin where they'd done it. Shortly after this operation he ran straight into a tree and knocked himself unconscious. He gave me a photograph of himself, taken in the park moments before this accident. It showed a dark-haired little boy, smiling a brave and hopeful smile, with the shadow of the future raised over him like a club. He had lived with another woman before me. They lived together for four or five years and then she moved to America. I could never get a sense of her, even though I'd seen photographs. We were both in our late twenties and it always seemed to me that we were dreaming: a membrane of unreality enclosed us. Our life together was strangely without sensation; and, even though he laid claim to a more definite range of feelings, when he spoke about them it was as if he were speaking about people that I'd never met. We bought a flat together, in the same part of London as he'd grown up in. His mother often came round and if her son was out she and I would sit and talk. She was very soft, his mother. Sometimes, looking at her gentle lap and cushiony bosom, I would feel a strong urge to lay my head on it. I loved her and I think that she loved me in return. She used to say that she hoped her son could hang on to me, as though I were a kite straining wildly in the wind at its tether. I didn't feel like that at all: most of the time, I felt as though I were in a trance-like sleep, like the slumbering princesses in the stories I used to read, who had reached out to touch the world with their innocent fingers and inadvertently drawn its poison.

One day my lover asked me whether I would like to have a baby, and it was then that I awoke. I did not want to do that. I made contact with this certainty as a tired swimmer, reaching the shallows, finally makes contact with the ocean floor, and like that swimmer I rose up out of the water walking, quickly gaining the dry bank of the beach while the old life ran off me in numberless rivulets and evaporated in the air.

It was at this time that I met Robert. I was thirty. I had moved into a flat of my own. I had been promoted at work and I was full of optimism and relief, like someone who has just recovered from an illness. I worked for a publisher of children's books, and one of the books that I had picked off the pile of manuscripts had done unexpectedly well. It was a story about a group of defective toys who decide one night to escape from the toy factory, where they've been thrown into a cardboard box. They climb through an open window and go out into the world to take their chances. Some of them creep into shop windows and hide behind the other toys. Some of them insinuate themselves into the beds of sleeping children. With their crooked eyes and badly sewn seams, they are looking for love. Robert told me that he had a four-year-old son and I was surprised but not put off. Nothing had yet happened to separate me from the world of my childhood: I was rooted in it still, like a neglected plant that runs yards of stalk for every bloom. There was something brutal about Robert's situation that appealed to me. I sensed that he disapproved of the way I had left my previous lover, and it was true that sometimes I thought of him as I had once, after I left, seen him, standing on the pavement outside my flat in the dark. I was closing the curtains and I happened to glance out. He meant me no harm; he was like a ghost, something you could have put your hand through. But the sight of him like that reminded me of the failure of my attempts at love. It filled me with feelings of disappointment. Over time my feelings fell away and the fact of the failure itself grew more distinct, as the cold disc of the moon grows distinct when the sun sinks.

Robert had many responsibilities and innumerable possessions – books, an estate car, a large collection of classical music, furniture, a cottage in the West Country. He was black-haired, with the flat, pale face of a monk. His blue eyes were the shape of almonds. His body was slender and fiercely hirsute. He had white teeth and big, clean hands that were always warm. At weekends, when Joseph came to stay, I would watch Robert bent on the tasks of fatherhood and something would open in me, a craving, like a fist unfolding in my chest. I could never watch Robert fixing a meal for Joseph, or washing his clothes or teaching him to play a game, without a thrill, a bird of panic and delight, beating about me. He wove me in, with those ministrations; he encompassed me in a spectacle of nurture so that sometimes I felt myself shrinking and becoming childlike while he grew larger, until he became an entire atmosphere.

I told my mother about Robert. One weekend we went, with Joseph, to visit my parents at their house, not the house I grew up in but a different house, in which my parents always seem to be temporarily accommodated and somehow unmanned, as if of their old power and its territories. In their kitchen, my parents and Robert stood in a group, large and iconic, like a set of vast, weathered statues. They greeted one another with the easy formality of neighbouring ambassadors. Later in the afternoon, my mother picked up Joseph and held him like a baby in her lap.

'You're very brave,' she said to me on the telephone, 'to be with a man who can never be completely yours.'

'I've got my own life,' I said.

'There's an easy way,' she stated, insinuatingly, 'to round that situation out.'

I first met Samantha when I was alone in Robert's flat. I didn't yet live there but I had my own keys and was often there when Robert was at work. I liked being in Robert's flat. Alone among his possessions I felt secure, as though Robert no longer existed; as though he had died and bequeathed me not just his things but his actual self. The sun would come in great slanting slabs through the glass in which dust would aimlessly spiral. The sofas and chairs, the pale rugs, the laden bookshelves stood immured in silence and sunlight, the relics of Robert. Yet I had, too, a sense of myself in those white rooms as a shadow, black, sharp-edged, immaterial, an infinitely projected stain. Some stubborn, resolute badness adhered to me, and in the rinsing columns of light I sought a form of transformation, a cleansing, for it had already become clear to me that I loved Robert helplessly and I prayed for a set of virtues that would prevent him from ever sending me away. The telephone rang and there was Robert's voice, winding down through the depths of the afternoon like the rope that connects ship to anchor. He said that he had been delayed and would be late. He had arranged for Samantha to drop Joseph at the flat. He hoped that was all right.

I was frightened of meeting Samantha, principally because I had had a dream in which I was lying in my bed in the dark while she attacked my prone body with a pair of scissors. She seemed, in the dream, to be both the instrument of a more generalised hatred and at the same time to be attacking me out of her own purpose, not because I had done anything wrong but because I was unlucky; because someone, I didn't know who, had failed to show the necessary vigilance in their care of me. The Samantha of my dream and the real Samantha didn't bear much physical resemblance to one another. My subconscious had constructed her out of aspects of Joseph's face combined with my memory of Roxanne's sister Stacy, with her curling lips and eyes.

When the doorbell rang, I opened it to find Joseph and a dark woman in dungarees standing there. She was slim and full-breasted, with dainty feet shod in Indian slippers. Her hair, which was long, was pulled back from her face by a silk scarf. She wore no make-up, or appeared not to. She had fine, white, slightly freckled skin and those features beloved of painters of the Renaissance – a small mouth, large, downcast eyes and a straight, fleshless nose that seemed perpetually to gesture to its own modest, chiselled extremity.

'Hello,' she said. 'At last.'

She was smiling all over her face, there in the doorway. She stood with her arm around Joseph. I noticed that Samantha bore a curious resemblance not only to her son but also to Robert himself. They were made in the same style. They were like a set of vases, or a series of paintings by a particular artist.

'Come in,' I said. Behind me Robert's rooms seemed inalienably his again, and I felt like an intruder who had foolishly answered the door.

'I've always loved this flat,' said Samantha, crossing the room on light feet to stand at the window.

'It's lovely,' I agreed.

'I've got a lot of criticisms of Robert,' she said, moving her gaze to the bookshelves, 'but he does have bloody good taste.'

She spoke in a clear, emphatic voice. What were these criticisms? I couldn't imagine – I thought Robert was irreproachable.

'What's your place like?' I asked.

'It's nothing,' stated Samantha. 'I don't want it to be anything. That's not what I'm about right now.'

She smiled and I smiled back as if I agreed that it wasn't what she was about.

'What about you?' she said. 'What do you want out of life?'

She sat down on the corner of the sofa and ran her fingers through Joseph's hair. He flipped over eagerly on to his back, urging his head into her hands, like a pet. He was five years old but around his mother he seemed to stray off the path of years, to become formless.

'I lived with somebody for a long time,' I said, as if by way of an explanation for my utter inability to answer her question.

'Were you married?'

'No.'

'Clever girl,' said Samantha. 'It's a lot easier to get into marriage than it is to get out. And you were sensible not to have a child. That's really the end. You're tied to each other for life after that. Although there are some wonderful things about it too – you don't want to miss out on it entirely.'

'No,' I said.

'I shouldn't think Robert wants to stop at one,' said Samantha. 'He'll give you a baby. He's a good father, good genes. You'll have to tear him away from that hospital, though, if you want any help. I could never manage it, but maybe you would. I've got a lot of intuition with fathers, and Robert's a good one. I was brought up by my father, and I'm telling you, *he* was terrible. My mother died when I was small –' I knew this already and therefore I said nothing '– so I have no memories of her at all, which I'm sure explains a lot. My father would never speak about her, not one word. If I asked he'd just get angry. I didn't even know what she looked like because he'd put away all the photographs. He was basically planning on just drinking himself to death, which he hasn't done yet, although he's well on his way, the old sod. A few years ago, though, I found those photographs. He'd stuffed them into a box in the back of a cupboard. I was on some kind of rampage – I don't remember why, I just remember being so bloody angry, and not caring what he did to me. I smashed up the house looking for them. Eventually I found the box and inside I found this photograph of a woman sitting on a beach holding a baby. I knew it was her because she looked exactly like me. She was wearing this old-fashioned bathing costume and a big hat. She was looking at the baby with this incredible expression on her face – just complete *adoration*. And for a moment I felt really jealous, I felt this red rage in my head, until I realised that it was me, that the baby must have been me. I remember saying to myself out loud, *She loved me.*' She whispered these words, gazing dramatically somewhere over my left shoulder. 'All those years I never knew, I just had this kind of blankness inside me, and then suddenly, there it was, this fact . . . Joe thinks I'm utterly mad because

I'm always telling him that I love him, but I just want him to be completely sure, *completely*, because I wasn't and I know that it damn well hurts. Every day, you have to say it. Every day.' She thumped the arm of the sofa. 'He just says, "I know, Mum." And I think, you don't know, you have no idea how *bloody* lucky you are.'

Robert did not return that day until late in the evening. Samantha had long gone. I remember that I gave Joseph his supper, and, although he was not usually hostile to me, on that occasion he sat silently at the table forcing food into his mouth with his hands, watching me with small, mean eyes as he did so. Leaving him there, I locked myself in the bathroom and cried. I cried often, in my life with Robert. As a child, too, I cried a lot, and so it has always seemed to me that these two parts of my life have occurred in the same geographical region, a place of wetness, of running rivers. Shortly after this meeting with Samantha I sold my flat and moved in with Robert. I had high hopes for those white rooms. In their purity I read messages of redemption. I felt that I had finally cast off my shadow, that I had leaped away from it as if over a chasm. Robert's life, so concrete, so definite, seemed to offer me a sanctuary from everything that teemed on the other side of that gap. When Joseph came to stay I felt his presence, too, as a kind of shield. He was a talisman, against a version of myself that had a way of making what was real unreal. At work, I published a story about a princess who could never grow old or die unless somebody fell in love with her. The problem was that, according to the spell, the instant someone fell in love with her he would perish. The princess roamed the world for hundreds of years, tired of her immortality and yet afraid of the love that promised to free her from it.

Robert did not particularly want to get married, it was clear. He didn't see the point. I could not explain to him my need to be possessed by him, nor the strange feeling I had that my parents still owned me, even though I saw them only a few times each year. My mother frequently asked whether Robert and I were ever going to marry, and the way she said it, as though it signified some lack of authenticity in Robert's feelings for me, filled me with anxiety. One day I told Robert, half jokingly, that if he wouldn't marry me I'd have to go and find somebody who would, and he looked surprised and not very amused and said that he'd think about it. Shortly afterwards we did marry. We were both thirty-three: we couldn't have expected it to make much difference that we were married, and at first it didn't, although later it became clear that our marrying was the first misunderstanding that led to our eventual estrangement.

In this period I was seeing rather a lot of my sister, Lucy, who lived in a house not far from Robert's flat with her husband Christian and their twin daughters. Lucy's girls were younger than Joseph, but nevertheless, my suddenly acquiring a child paved the way for one of the periods of closeness we intermittently have, when we unexpectedly find our different roads meeting at a junction. Lucy had not gone on to live the life that her endeavours at school and university had indicated. When we were in our twenties she confided to me that more than anything she wanted to be a mother. I was surprised by this: I felt nothing of that kind myself. It was as if the desire had been conferred on her by a random process of selection, or as if it were the summons of an irresistible cult. She laid aside her ambitions and achievements and quietly donned the selfless white robe of parenthood.

People have always commented on the striking differences between Lucy and me, both physically and in our personalities. They expect us as twins to mirror one another, whereas actually our dissimilarities are so uncompromising that we are like two people who have been created from the division of one. It is for this reason, perhaps, that we have avoided each other in adulthood. For each of us, the sight of the other reminds us of what we lack, and can give rise to the unpleasant suspicion that these qualities were not fairly bestowed but were stolen. Lucy, for example, has countless friends, a whole group who go to parties and dinners and on holiday together, while I have no talent for friendship. I, on the other hand, have no fear of ideas, whereas Lucy can be made unhappy by the mere mention of a notion with which she disagrees. Lucy is a person who experiences emotion within the pressure of an inner constriction. Just as sometimes the wind blows more violently when it passes through a tunnel, so Lucy's feelings seem to roar in her narrow passages. The sight of her moved either to joy or to sadness is nearly unbearable, so primitive is this mechanism of hers. Usually she blocks it off: she has ordered her life so as to avoid extremes of emotion. Instead she has cultivated, like a thorny hedge around herself, a suspicious nature. You always prick yourself on Lucy, even if you don't notice it at the time. You find the scratches later – they don't hurt, but you see them.

When Robert had to work at weekends, I would often go with Joseph round to Lucy's house. Lucy felt sorry for Joseph, and for me, but for different reasons. It must be *so* difficult, she would say, squeezing her eyelids together. I never asked her what she thought the difficulty was, but I imagine she would have said something about my having the responsibility for a child but none of the pleasure. For a person like Lucy, love is like an oxygen tank that sustains her at the unbreathable depths at which she lives. It is an artificial arrangement that permits her survival in a submerged world. It was often after returning from an afternoon spent with Joseph at Lucy's house that I found it easiest to love him. Ambling along the rattling, fume-filled London pavements I would relish the bloodless lightness of our bond – it seemed all preference, all civility, after that family house with its matching faces and importunate bodies, its patriotic clutter, its pall of observance and association beneath which I always seemed to hear a ceaseless grinding, as if of the machinery of life.

Lucy at that time was very preoccupied by a weekly newspaper column in which the writer – like Lucy, the mother of small children – described her family life in the framework of a soap opera, a narrative more concerned with continuance than with arrival at a particular destination and which, while maintaining a resemblance to life, travelled unerringly through the issues of the day. I had already heard of this column before Lucy mentioned it to me. It was to become famous, and her interest provided the proof of its popularity. I could never get around to reading it myself, although everyone said how amusing it was. It would not be an exaggeration to say that Lucy was fixated, both by the column and by the woman, Serena Porter, who wrote it. As I understood it, Serena Porter's success lay in her ability to depict the travails of ordinary women in a glamorous manner. She made them feel that they wanted to be as they already were. She insinuated herself beneath the carapace of female doubt and constructed a fiction of domestic glory there. This sort of thing is a mystery to me, the fervid weighing-up that people like Lucy go in for. Why did it make so much difference, that she believed this woman to be just like her? The only answer I could think of was that it was because, in fact, the woman wasn't like her at all.

Anyway, one afternoon I turned up at Lucy's house with Joseph to find her in a state of agitation. It seemed that Serena Porter, the columnist, had disclosed in that day's column that her husband was dying of cancer.

'That's sad,' I said, following her into the kitchen.

'Isn't it awful?' she said. 'Their children are three and one!'

Lucy often spoke in what was to me a sort of code. Her kitchen, with its rows of unwashed beakers and moulded plastic bowls, its crumb-strewn surfaces and walls hung with chaotic children's paintings, was like the site of a lost military campaign. It did not at all resemble the kitchen of our childhood. It was at once suggestive of far greater effort and more resounding failure than the rooms in which we grew up.

'It's just so depressing,' she continued, turning smartly away to put the kettle on. 'All afternoon I've been sitting here thinking, What's the point? What's the point of having things if they can just be taken away from you like that? Mum is devastated,' she added. 'I spoke to her earlier.'

'Is she?' I said, bewildered.

'You know, the funny thing was that when I read it the first thing I thought was, Well, at least it wasn't one of the children. I think that if one of my children died, I wouldn't actually be able to cope. Whereas, if it was Christian, I mean, I'd never be happy again but I'd go on living. Anyway, I said this to Mum on the phone and we had this sort of *argument*, because she felt very strongly that your husband dying was far worse than your child.'

I saw that Lucy was wrestling with emotion. Joseph and I watched her wrestle, there in the kitchen. Her broad, un-exceptional face was like a window that is never cleaned, smeared by tiredness and tedium. Behind that window, it seemed, moral struggles occurred, equivalences were sought, a life of flesh was worked into a life of reason. I was reminded in that moment how completely Lucy was occupied by this labour, which was ongoing and could never be completed, and which was perennially in a state of imminent reversion to its basic constituents – two children and a man, who sometimes seemed to me to have ransacked Lucy's mind while she was away consulting her heart, to have devoured it by increments, like mice burrowing in a larder.

'I didn't say this, but I wasn't sure she was being *completely* honest,' said Lucy. Her voice had risen several registers and her cheeks were red.

'Why wouldn't she be?'

'I don't know,' said Lucy. 'I think it was meant as some kind of criticism.'

'Of you?'

'Of the idea that you might love your children more. Joseph, would you like to go and watch television with the girls? They're in the other room. If they're standing right in front of the screen then just lift them out of the way.'

'OK,' said Joseph.

He got up to go, although I could tell that he wanted to stay and listen to our conversation. Joseph always attended to the talk of adults. It was as though he thought he might hear something that would explain what had happened to him.

'Is that all right?' I said.

'Yeah,' he said.

I worried a great deal about whether Joseph was happy when he was with me. I never knew what was the right thing to do with him; there were no nerves, no instincts to tell me.

'She's really just talking about herself,' continued Lucy. 'Her idea of a proper marriage is one where your husband comes first and your children second. When she was here the other week, she was really shocked that I didn't go and put make-up on before Christian came home.'

I laughed.

'But your feelings *do* change when you have children. I'm sure Christian would say exactly the same thing. You can't just carry on being the way you were.'

'Why not?' I said.

'You just can't,' said Lucy. 'The children take priority.'

'Are you saying,' I ventured, 'that having a child affects your capacity to love other people?'

'Yes, in a way,' said Lucy. 'It's just that they need you so much, and you'd do anything for them, I mean anything. After that, there isn't much room for anyone else. It's a very selfless kind of love,' she added.

'Isn't it the opposite? Isn't it a form of self-love?'

'It's difficult to understand if you don't have children,' said Lucy. 'I remember, when the twins were born, looking at them and having this amazing moment of realisation – that these two tiny people were more important than I was.'

'More important to who? To yourself?'

'That's what it's like,' said Lucy. 'I don't think I've ever felt that about a man. But the children belong to both of you, so at least you've got that in common. I remember thinking, God, why all this fuss about romantic love! This is *much* bigger! I used to really worry about it, but these days I just think, Why? Why struggle against it? Christian and I had our time together, and now we've got the children – and they've made me happier than anything else in the world.'

It had to be admitted that she didn't look particularly happy.

'So what I say about Serena Porter,' she concluded, 'is that it's very sad, but she'll live.'

On our way home I asked Joseph whether he liked going to Lucy's house.

'Not really,' he said. 'There's nothing for me to do. I always just get left with the children.'

I saw less of Lucy after that. Her judgement of Serena Porter was, however, correct: she did live. She continued to write, some said brilliantly, about her husband's illness and eventual death, after which there was a silence that seemed to me somewhat scripted, like the orchestrated pause in a piece of music, before, as it seemed by common consent, her long-running account of family life resumed.

But my conversation with Lucy stayed in my mind, and grew clearer and more emphatic as time passed. I may have mocked the little games of life and death she played with herself, but in a different way I played them too. I had begun to see evidence, in nearly all his actions, that Robert loved Joseph more than me. In the street it was Joseph's hand he reached for, not mine; returning from work, Joseph was the one he hugged and kissed. These actions, harmless in them-selves, nevertheless taunted me with the spectre of thwarted possession. In them, I saw my life passing unwitnessed; I felt a terrible despair at having failed to find another human being to corroborate my existence. I wanted a relationship in which love given was equal to love received. I wanted something of my own.

'Do you think we'll ever have a child?' I asked him, driving down to the cottage late one night with Joseph asleep in the back.

We had been married for about three years. Neither of us had mentioned having children before, and this in itself had come to seem increasingly suspicious to me. A baby, I thought, would solve everything. It would even things out. We would have a child each. It was only fair.

'I've already got a child,' said Robert, staring straight through the window at the ghostly snaking road.

'But I don't.'

'You never said you wanted one.'

'Well, I do.'

We had several conversations like this one, and then several more in which Robert's objections became clearer and clearer, as though bandages were being lifted off to reveal at their centre a still-tender wound. He said that he didn't want to go through all that again. He said that his life was as he wanted it. He said that he had enough on his hands. It had been too difficult, the last time. He said that he would understand if I found his position unacceptable – he hadn't known himself how deeply he felt until I'd brought the subject up. Couldn't we be happy, he said, as we were?

Samantha, meanwhile, had come into some family money, and opened a flower shop in South Kensington. It was a great success. I went there one afternoon to return Joseph and found Samantha camouflaged amid the wet, scented foliage, her hair gathered up on her head.

'This is the only decent love you ever get,' she said to me, grinning, as Joseph flung his arms around her aproned waist and pressed his face mutely against her chest.

That night I wept and raged at Robert and he lay beside me like a figure carved of stone, helpless. My thirty-seventh birthday came and went.

'You'll have to get a move on now,' said my mother, on the telephone.

It was at the flower shop that Samantha met Harry. Harry was a figure of obstinate stability. He was aristocratic and wealthy and said very little. A fog of vague geniality enveloped him. His marked face suggested that somewhere in his life he had neutered himself, blown a circuit – nothing Samantha did or said could rouse the dead nerves of his idiotic good nature. It turned out they were perfectly suited. They got married, and shortly afterwards Samantha announced that she was pregnant. She produced a daughter and, a year later, another. She and Harry bought a house in the south of France and spent holidays there.

Walking back to the flat one evening, I met my previous lover in the street. He had hardly changed. Nor, he said, had I. We had both just turned forty. This fact, there in the street, seemed incredible to me, although I didn't say so. Looking into my old lover's face I felt myself travelling along a strange loop of time, so that everything that had happened since we parted seemed all at once to have been a dream. It seemed that I had only to link arms with him to find that I had woken up and become myself again, that these years I had lived with Robert were mere projections of my subconscious anxiety.

'Are you still in the same place?' he asked.

'Yes.'

'With, was it Robert? And the boy – what was his name?'

'Joseph.'

'Joseph,' repeated my old lover, sighing and looking up at the dark, brown sky. 'I've thought about him a lot, over the years.'

'Have you?'

'In some way I felt jealous of him. The last time I met you in the street,' he continued, 'you were with him.'

I had forgotten it, but this was true. It was shortly after Robert and I had started living together. I was still happy, dashing across the road holding Joseph's hand, and when I saw my old lover standing there I had felt a cruel relief, as though he were floating on a boat far out at sea, a boat I had escaped through some selfish but necessary act, leaving him there while I gained the mainland, the bustling concourses of life.

'I thought, How can she love someone else's child but not me?'

'What are you doing now?' I said.

'Oh, much the same. No changes really. I was unhappy for a long time,' he added challengingly, 'but I'm feeling a lot better these days.'

So I was reminded that that time, too, had been a dream, a numb enclosure, and suddenly my whole life stretched behind me, annexe after annexe, to form a soft transparent tunnel. I returned home. Robert was not there. I walked around the flat looking at its objects. They were the same objects I had looked at during those first, solitary sunlit afternoons, when they had awed me so, because I had thought that I was arriving in this world at the moment of its flowering, in the midst of its opportunities; when really, like someone visiting an art gallery not knowing that it is about to close for the day, I was seeing them in their twilight and got a mere glimpse of rooms full of beauty before the doors began to close, one after another, and these treasures were left to their dark hours of silent sleep.

I wondered whether I would tell Robert about my meeting with my old lover, but when he returned from work he was silent and solemn-faced. Presently he told me that Samantha had announced her intention of moving permanently to France, taking Joseph with her. He had offered to keep Joseph here, but Joseph wanted to go.

'I don't know, perhaps we should have had children after all,' said Robert, sighing and rubbing his face with his large white hands, 'He might have felt that we were more of a proper family.'

I turned my back to him and began to cry.

Once I'd walked around Fulford, I turned and went back up the lane to the house. The sun had come out and people were venturing into their gardens with watering cans and trowels and folding chairs. I'd thought of asking Lucy to come with me to see the old place, but these days she was busy. When the twins went to school she'd got a job in television. Now she supports the family while Christian stays at home writing a book that he hopes one day to have published. My mother was distressed by this turn of events – Christian's career in the City was her pride and joy. Nevertheless, I have the impression that Lucy has freed herself. She has acquired a quality of authenticity before which the past retreats and grows dim, so that it is the background, drawn in broad strokes, of whatever image she chooses to impose on it.

Robert and I had just separated, that summer of 20–. At around the same time my father fell ill. It wasn't a serious illness, but even so Lucy and I were concerned for my mother and about the work of looking after him that fell to her. My mother insisted that she was quite able to do it. One evening I telephoned her to say that I was thinking of taking some time off work. I offered to come down and stay with them for a while. Oh no, said my mother in a panicked voice, that really won't be necessary. I understood then that she was frightened of me: that for all these years she'd worried that one day the world would return me to her, like an object that has been found to be faulty. I wanted to ask her what she'd done to me; I wanted the secret knowledge that only she possessed. It's so sad about you and Robert, she said then. I was sad about Robert too, but strangely it was Joseph that I missed. My palms prickled with the habit of touching him. The absence of his narrow white body was like a hole bored into the ground just beside me. I would think of him with his little sisters and a feeling that was half pleasure and half pain would spread across my chest.

You should have had children, my mother said. You young women these days, you're so busy with your careers that you put it off and put if off until it's too late. The moment was never right, I said. You can't wait for the right moment, she said. You never know what's going to happen. Look at me, she said, I always thought I'd have six children, but life doesn't always go according to plan.

I didn't know you wanted more children, I said.

Oh, I did, she replied.

Why didn't you have them? I said. What happened?

She was silent.

We didn't know you were there, she said then. They thought there was just one baby. By the time they realised there were two they had to act quickly. Something went wrong and so they removed my womb. It was a great sadness, she said. Your father and I desperately wanted a son. But as I say, life doesn't always go according to plan.

I reached the end of the drive and there was the house again, sitting in sunshine now. While I watched the front door opened and a lady came out. She was somewhere in her fifties, with dark hair that was going grey. She was wearing a long skirt and a light-coloured shirt and she had a basket of gardening tools in her hand. She started to work on one of the flowerbeds at the front of the house. A light wind got up and stirred the warming air, pushing the lady's skirt gently to one side. Presently a man, her husband, came out. He had a mug in his hand and he gave it to her. Looking around the garden I could see no evidence of children – perhaps they had grown up and gone away. If that was the case then this couple would have plenty of spare rooms. They probably slept in the large room overlooking the back garden, where my parents used to sleep. My room, which was smaller, would be free. I was sure that this couple, who seemed so nice, wouldn't mind me going up there to take a look. I would go in and I would close the door. And sitting on the bed I would hear all the little sounds around me, the sounds of people in other rooms, the sound of the television on downstairs and supper being cooked in the kitchen and the table being laid. I would sit on my bed as the afternoon turned outside the window to night. I would wait for them to call me down.

Mrs Daley's Daughter

Mrs Daley was surprised to discover that at sixty-one she felt more oppressed by the pointlessness of a Tuesday morning than she had at any other time in her life. She did not make this discovery, nor analyse its significance, through any deliberate scientific process. It was rather that she would occasionally become aware, in the midst of her consciousness, of a certain change in outside conditions, a certain quality to the silence, as someone acting on a stage might become aware that the audience had departed; and she experienced doubt, in these moments, as to whether she should go on acting her part or merely stop. The kitchen clock might stand at half past ten for hours when a morning took this turn; her appetite for life, her interest, which was the interest of someone standing very close to something, in every aspect of its texture, vanished so entirely that she could not even remember what it was that had propelled her through time to this point.

Mrs Daley felt very sorry for herself at such times: she brought the sentimentality of a mother to her situation, except in reverse, for now it was she who was the lost child, and corresponding tears of sympathy would spring to her eyes. Just as her children used to call for her when the thread of things, for one reason or another, had slipped from their hands, so it was her habit now to turn to them to get the day's faltering drama back on the road. The small taste of power these communications yielded was enough to start her heart beating again and cause the hands of the clock to turn once more; but they could leave her, too, with a debt, a sort of hangover, depending on the quality of the fix. Mrs Daley's telephone, through which this fix was obtained, had not long before been out of order for a week, with the men failing to come and then coming and failing to repair it, and Mrs Daley had descended into the grip of passions she was unable to control. She had run around the village, dishevelled by rain and wind, with the news of her catastrophe: if she couldn't speak to her telephone herself, her only recourse was to speak about it to other people. On and on she talked until, as if watching these conversations from afar, she became aware that the thing she feared so deeply that she could never permit herself to suspect it – that people might laugh at her – was in fact happening before her eyes, and still she could not stop. Towards the end of that week something else happened, which was that a sensation of peace, almost of bodily lightness, descended on Mrs Daley. For a day or two she ceased to harry time and a new delight adhered to the business of living. She felt inconsequent and free, so that by the time the men fixed the telephone she might not have cared whether they did so or not, had she not known herself better.

The village lay at the bottom of a large hollow in the south of England; hills rose steeply to all sides of it, so that the horizon was entirely encircled by a high ridge on which, in fading light, a line of trees formed an unbroken edging of black. To leave Ravenley in any direction required climbing one of these hills and then descending the other side, when a view of the forgotten plains of the outside world could be obtained, glittering, despoiled, crawling with life. Ravenley was composed of twenty or so houses which stood at different angles around a narrow lane, a grouping which seemed arbitrary and somehow human, as though some old curse had transfixed it in time, condemning it to an eternity of momentary conversance. At weekends, tourist traffic would tentatively ply the lane; unfamiliar faces would stare out through the windows of cars, as though with the expectation that some malevolent transaction was about to occur. All sorts of people passed through Ravenley in this way: elderly couples, grey and erect and unspeaking; families whose muffled chaos pressed at the glass; young lovers, girls with long hair and lipstick, men in sunglasses, who touched each other and said things smilingly, privately. They rarely stopped, not even to visit the church, which was Saxon, and listed in *Notable Churches of England*. They passed by, disappointed and relieved, as people on a boat might pass by a paradisiacal island on which they had discerned evidence of human settlement.

Ravenley had no pub or shop, no car park or playground, not even a telephone box. Superficially, it had not changed in a hundred years. The world beyond it sustained this appearance in the way that a life-support machine sustains the sleep of a dead patient. It was a costly process that had no purpose beyond the consolation of certain feelings. On the other side of the hill different standards obtained. Electricity pylons marched across grey, cluttered fields. Housing developments rose bloodily from the earth. Roads and roundabouts, petrol stations, landfill sites, industrial estates and shopping centres, all at different stages in a cycle of decay, gave the impression of something injured, something mutilated perhaps beyond repair, but for the time being at least independently alive. Cars issued discreetly from Ravenley's well-tended properties, ascended to the horizon and disappeared, to return again later, freighted with food and fuel. These properties, so unmarked, seemed like embodiments of pure emotion. Detached from their material shame, with no discernible edge of need, they gave the impression of housing lives in which fact was recessive and feeling predominant, in which feeling might have attained the status of fact, and become the moderating force of daily existence.

The church was cold inside and the colour of old bone. Narrow wooden stalls stood in rows along either side. When the sun came out, spirals of dust whirled aimlessly in its beams. In the small vestry, spiders' webs had dried in matted layers over the mullioned window-panes. The vicar, who dispensed services to parishes all around the area and was therefore, like a man maintaining a deception, always in a hurry, stood in the vestry fortnightly for the few seconds it took him to struggle out of his cassock, leaving the door open while he lifted it precipitately over his head and making his escape as the small, coughing congregation continued to face the abandoned altar. Some of the residents kept a rota for ringing the church bell. At night its arhythmic tolling could sometimes be heard, a phenomenon for which there were explanations, although in the past it had signified a death.

The road, pitted, crusty, splitting, sluiced with mud and water, came winding down the hill, ran past the church and meandered back up the other side. It was so narrow that if two cars met at a bend they were almost certain to collide. The residents of Ravenley drove fast, or badly, along this road, as they did not along the bigger, marked road that met it at either end at the top of the hill. It was as though, journeying around this tributary, they believed themselves unwatched; they assumed the status of a private thought, travelling impenetrably through the burrows of a brain. Sometimes large holes would appear in the road, or, in summer, patches of grass, and in winter its steeply sloping parts could freeze over so that the village was entirely cut off from the warm, diesel-smelling places that ruminated in their imperturbable life a mere four or five miles away. Nobody liked it when this happened, suggestive as it was of neglect, or inconsequence. Telephone calls to the council were made. Unseen people occasionally brought their junk, their old sofas and dilapidated kitchen units, and placed it in piles in the fields running along the road just outside the village. Once or twice, boys from the local town had burned stolen cars in the woods, and their tarry, half-melted skeletons remained there. The road invited these disburdenings: it didn't seem to belong to the world of laws and reprisals; it was confessional and private; it was defenceless. This fact made certain people angry. The road was a form of consciousness, a necessary torment: it was what conferred existence upon Ravenley and what caused it pain.

People moved in and out and these changes – some to the good, some less so – were absorbed, altering the organism only slowly and mostly imperceptibly, because the houses in Ravenley were expensive and the unstable phase of life tended to be lived elsewhere. Children grew up and left and news of them came back like news of a distant war in which they were fighting and from which they were occasionally permitted leave, when they would return for a week or two to wander about as though in a mirage of the past. It often seemed that while they had changed Ravenley had not, but by the time they left that impression had usually been reversed. Money lay like a new stratum, the dramatic evidence of a recent geological event, over everything – it caused a perceptual delay while it was dug through. The houses in Ravenley were full of heat and light, of appliances and new carpets and fresh paintwork, and it took time, required an adjustment of the eyes, as if to darkness, to see the old familiar things. They were there, but in less visible detail.

Mrs Daley lived at Hill House, a square flint building that stood on an incline at the fringes of the village. It was a house of several rooms: as if they were paying guests, Mrs Daley discharged her duties towards these rooms with pride but without undue affection. The kitchen was where she spent her time; it was here, in a high-backed wooden chair adjacent to the kettle, that the drug of conversation was procured. This drug was constituted in its strongest form in the person of her daughter Josephine, and so, while her other children might encounter her in lighter moods, Mrs Daley's conversations with Josephine were generally conducted from her position at the bottom of the deepest pit of anomie a Tuesday morning could offer. Josephine's combination of sensitivity and stubbornness made her easy to wound while unlikely to admit it, but her life also tended to the dramatic, so that a call to Josephine had to have plenty of space and time around it in which her mother's feelings about her latest activity could have the opportunity to unfold. Some of these feelings, being impossible to resolve, acted as storylines that persisted, without ever strictly progressing, through a whole series of calls. If new and more compelling feelings emerged these standard lines could be allowed to fade into the background, but could be worked back up at any time. It was a delicate business, though; it was strong stuff to handle. There had been long periods of silence between Mrs Daley and her daughter. It was important, as it was not with her other children, that Josephine should know that she, Mrs Daley, was a human being. Josephine caused her real feeling, of an unpleasant sort. That feeling was guilt, and it had the effect on Mrs Daley of making her believe that she was Josephine's victim. Nothing she had done had ever been good enough for Josephine; it was usually with this thought that Mrs Daley would withdraw into hurt isolation, from which she meditated continually on whether her silence had yet achieved its aim, which was to punish her daughter.

Such punishments had become somewhat harder to administer since Josephine had taken up with Roger and moved both practically and spiritually so far out of Mrs Daley's territory that she felt uncertain, as she did when abroad, of her own pronouncements and mannerisms. From her perch in the village of Ravenley Mrs Daley had attempted to keep abreast of Josephine's movements in London, where at one moment she had been engaged to a perfectly nice – though somehow, as Mrs Daley now regretted having mentioned to her friends, not quite right – lawyer called David, and at the next had moved in with Roger, whose marriage Mrs Daley suspected her of disrupting. Roger was some sort of artist. He had two small children who seemed to spend rather more time with him than was usual or, given the circumstances, desirable. In the early days, stiff with disapproval, she would telephone Josephine and be so deafened by the menagerie sounds in the background, and by the new evidence of struggle in Josephine's voice, that blank, protective feelings would spring up in her, so redolent of emergency did the whole thing seem. She had usually called to joust, but the situation clearly permitted a new frankness. She once enquired as to where their mother was, and received the shocking reply that Josephine didn't know. Somewhere in France, it seemed, travelling. Roger was preparing for a show, whatever that meant, which left Josephine looking after two children who had nothing to do with her. With a sense of herself coming to the fore, Mrs Daley offered to find a nanny for them. We can't afford a nanny, Josephine replied; and besides, she continued after a pause, they've had enough disruption already. We can't start leaving them with a complete stranger. This was the old territory, the old turf. Mrs Daley felt its familiar tread beneath her feet, and so she permitted herself to say, by-the-by, that David, the abandoned lawyer, seemed to be doing awfully well; she'd read about a case of his on the front page of the newspaper. Did she still see him at all?

Josephine had been living with Roger now for a year. His ex-wife remained on holiday, having been taken to court and for reasons Mrs Daley could not establish lost custody of her children. (How much easier, she sometimes thought, how much better it would look if she had simply died!) David, the lawyer, had continued to go from strength to strength. The things that Mrs Daley had disliked in him – his aversion to money (a lawyer!), his unseemly devotion to certain causes, terrorists and immigrants and what have you – now had the benefit of being seen in a new light, the light of modern sympathies which Mrs Daley had been forced to acquire by Josephine's unconventional behaviour. She had met Roger's children, a boy of five and a girl of three, several times, and had turned upon them the full force of her charitable nature. From Roger, his wife, and even from

Josephine herself, except in her saintly role as their carer, she was obliged to avert her eyes; but for those children, '*those children*' as she in hushed and reverent tones referred to them among her acquaintance, and for David, she reserved unshakeable sympathy. They were among the good, the poor, the innocent of the earth. They were the new martyrs; when she spoke of broken families, her friends knew that, sadly, she now did so from experience.

Further trials, however, awaited Mrs Daley's good nature and openness to change. Josephine had become pregnant; the birth was a matter of weeks away. Mrs Daley delighted in grandchildren – she had several already – in the usual context; she liked to see her children tied down by *their* children; she had a sense of it all as a great tapestry being embroidered away into the future. The correct weaving of this tapestry, however, depended on certain conventions – not many, for heaven knew she was no stick in the mud, but a few! – being observed. That Josephine and Roger were not married, and had no intention of doing so, breached one such convention. That they were poor, and lived in conditions approximating squalor, breached another. The matter of those children, Roger's children, presented to Mrs Daley's happiness another obstacle, which she was obliged for the sake of contradiction to keep more or less to herself: the fact was that no matter how heartbreaking she found them, she did not mistake them for members of her family. She could, artistically speaking, accept Josephine devoting her life to their care; what she could not accept was that that situation should have any new issue. To produce a baby in the midst of it was to confuse two things, the first being a life in which sins and sadnesses were atoned for by unstinting good works, the second being the more normal way, in which two innocent people created other innocent beings. The first kind of life Mrs Daley vaguely felt to be a life of ideas, of the intellect, and in her mind it was suited to Josephine, who was so complicated and independent and had the habit, too, of exonerating her faults with selfless, disinterested labour. Mrs Daley could accept this life, as she accepted all forms of art, so long as it had no real and personal consequences. Visiting Josephine, and seeing her clearly pregnant body, she had been afflicted by feelings of shock, almost of distaste. She had never before, on seeing a pregnant woman, related her condition to the sexual act, but she related it now, and it all seemed to point back to her, Mrs Daley, with long, accusing fingers. The sadness of it was, Mrs Daley said to herself, that by mixing all these things together everything was spoiled, feelings were tainted. She found herself quite out of patience with Roger's children, and possessed of the conviction, before she had even laid eyes on it, that Josephine's baby would perhaps not be her favourite grandchild.

'I was clearing out the back room,' said Josephine, when Mrs Daley had dialled her number and made the observation that she had been a long time answering. Josephine spoke in a voice that was high and young-sounding and belied her predicament. 'We're turning it into a little office for me.'

'What for?' Mrs Daley gave a mirthless laugh. 'You won't be working once the baby comes. And anyway,' she added, when it seemed Josephine was to make no reply, 'I thought you were going to turn that into the nursery.'

Josephine, in fact, had never stated such an intention. Mrs Daley had suggested it on her recent visit and been vaguely rebuffed by Josephine saying that they 'didn't know what they were going to do with it yet', a form of words in which many aspects of Josephine and Roger's life these days found expression and which irritated Mrs Daley beyond her power to disguise it.

'No,' said Josephine, in a surprised voice. 'I never said that.'

'Well where,' persisted Mrs Daley, 'is the baby going to sleep?'

'With us,' said Josephine, surprised again, as if she didn't know where else Mrs Daley expected such sleep to occur.

'With you?' parried Mrs Daley. Her blood was up, her heart was beating once more. The kitchen clock stood at nearly eleven, and counting. 'You can't have a baby in your bed!'

There was a moment of silence on the other end. In her kitchen, with her weapons lined up awaiting the trigger of her daughter's reply, Mrs Daley had a brief and peculiar sensation of falling.

'Well,' said Josephine, in a friendly tone, 'we'll see. I expect you're right. How's everything down there? How's Dad?'

Mrs Daley, who had not thought of her husband since last seeing him at eight-thirty that morning, was forced to answer that he was fine; but Josephine's changed manner was stuck in her chest like a knife. Her offer of confrontation had been rejected: such a thing had rarely, if ever, happened before. What was the meaning of it? She opened her mouth to ask but Josephine rained blow after blow upon her, enquiring after the weather, the garden, the evening course she was taking in watercolour painting, and it wasn't until she asked about the Porters and how they were settling into Ravenley that Mrs Daley had the chance to strike back.

'Oh!' she exclaimed. 'They're the most lovely family! It's such a boon for the village that they've decided to live here permanently, although I can't say I'm surprised – London really isn't the place to bring up small children. All that dirt and noise!'

'It must be nice to have some younger people around,' said Josephine. 'Some new blood.'

'You make us sound like a pack of vampires!' cried Mrs Daley. 'We're far from second best for people like the Porters, you know. You should see what the houses here cost now!'

'I know,' said Josephine. 'It's awful.'

'I don't see what's so awful about it,' said Mrs Daley. 'If people have worked hard all their lives they've got the right to some peace and quiet.'

'What are they like, anyway?' said Josephine. 'The Porters.'

'They're a very interesting couple,' confided Mrs Daley. 'He's a lawyer – I've been meaning to ask him if he knows David. I'm sure they've bumped into each other on the circuit. And her – well, you know all about her.'

'I know she writes a column,' said Josephine. 'But I don't think I've ever read it.'

'Oh, it's all the rage!' said Mrs Daley. 'They're talking about it up and down the country. Poor girl, I should think she's been knocked flat by all the attention!'

'I'm sure she loves it,' said Josephine. 'Why would she do it otherwise?'

'She's not really *like* that,' said Mrs Daley consideringly. 'She's had rather a sad life. When you look at her your heart just goes out to her, she's such a fragile little thing. I can see that I'm going to become very fond of her,' she continued, feeling through the silence, the darkness of the telephone, her daughter's insecure sensibility, as a pianist might feel the keyboard. 'She's about your age, probably, rather beautiful and terribly clever. To look at her you'd never know she'd had two children – I imagine that she had London at her feet! But she couldn't bear the idea of the children growing up there. She said to me the other day, Barbara, I just want them to have a *proper* childhood, like your children must have had. She's got very strong opinions but you'd never know it, she's such a charming, feminine person.'

This account did not strictly correspond with what Mrs Daley actually thought of Serena, or whatever she called herself, whose beauty and success, being of a type that did not accord with Mrs Daley's taste, did not for a moment recommend her, and whose opinions marked her out as a positive danger. Her report of Serena's comments similarly bore the stamp of invention; if anything, Mrs Daley had the impression from what she had heard that Serena was disappointed by Ravenley, hankered to return to London and before long probably would, which fleeting quality suited her for Mrs Daley's fictional purposes. She had had high hopes for Josephine, once: the person she described as Serena Porter was in fact a compromise between these hopes and the actual possibilities Josephine offered.

'She sounds interesting,' said Josephine, and Mrs Daley, hearing, she thought, hurt in her voice, felt the dip and wing of triumph and then the strange flood of tender concern. She readied herself for the next phase, in which she would take pity on her prey, bombard her with solicitations, and extract from her the prize of self-revelation.

'Oh, she is!' she exclaimed.

'What's the matter?' said Josephine.

Mrs Daley was so rarely asked this question that it immediately occurred to her to answer *everything*. Josephine was not, however, speaking to her – she had merely neglected to put her hand over the receiver. There was a crash in the background and then a child's crying and to her dejection and surprise Josephine said, 'Sorry, Mum, I've got to go,' and then she was gone.

It was only directly after conversations such as this that Mrs Daley recalled that the victory she pursued in them so energetically did not, in fact, exist. Even when she got the better of Josephine she felt only sadness afterwards, a sadness that set in like rain, with her love for Josephine something left outside in it. But it was not in her nature to brood on such curious glimpses of her life as she sometimes, in this form, received. She merely rearranged her pieces, advancing some, retracting others, and waited for Mr Daley to come in, when she would inform him of the state of play.

Three weeks later Mr and Mrs Daley were in their car, driving to London on a cold autumn morning to visit their daughter. This visit had not taken place with quite the alacrity Mrs Daley's friends, or her husband, had expected. Its motivation – the arrival of Josephine's baby – had been in place for several days. All Mrs Daley could offer by means of an explanation for the delay was that Josephine's baby had arrived rather earlier than she, Mrs Daley, had anticipated, and that she could not be expected just to drop everything. She was a busy person; she had made plans.

'The seats,' she observed, 'don't seem to be as comfortable as they were.'

'The seats,' Mr Daley replied, 'are exactly the same.'

They were on the motorway, going very fast. Mr Daley pulled out unexpectedly to overtake a small van from whose exhaust a black plume of smoke projected, and was greeted by a fanfare of horns. Mrs Daley watched the van drift backwards past her window, strangely close, as if it were being washed away.

'All I know,' she said, shifting in her seat and causing herself a sharp intake of breath, 'is that I'm losing sensation in my leg and we've only been in the car –' she consulted her watch – 'for just over twenty minutes.'

'This is a brand-new model of the same car,' said Mr Daley. 'If anything, the seats will be more comfortable.'

'They seem harder.'

'If anything,' Mr Daley repeated, 'they'll be more comfortable.'

Mrs Daley observed a silence, during which she turned this way and that and probed the carpeted space at her feet as if hoping that it would miraculously enlarge. Straightening her leg in a diagonal direction, she winced and gasped.

'I'm sorry,' she said to her husband.

'We'll have to turn around,' he dramatically replied, removing his hands from the steering wheel and then replacing them, apparently with the intention of executing this manoeuvre there and then across the three busy lanes of the motorway. 'We have at least another hour in the car. Please tell me if you would like me to turn around,' he added, after a pause.

'All I know,' Mrs Daley repeated, 'is that I'm getting shooting pains down my leg.'

'You can recline the seat,' stated Mr Daley flatly. 'This is a brand-new car. The seats recline.'

Mrs Daley sighed and groped around at the base of the seat.

'There is a dial on your left-hand side,' said Mr Daley. 'If you turn this dial, the seat will recline.'

'I'm trying to turn it,' puffed Mrs Daley.

'It's a calibrated dial,' said Mr Daley. 'If you force it, you will break it.'

'I'm not going to break it,' said Mrs Daley. 'Perhaps you should do it, if you're worried.'

'I am driving,' Mr Daley replied, without turning his head.

Looking out of the window, Mrs Daley observed the tundra of warehouses and car parks and petrol stations and electricity cables that constituted the view

'It's so sad,' she said, 'what they've done to the country-side.'

Mrs Daley permitted herself on occasion to make revolutionary remarks such as this, knowing that her husband would contradict her on any social, political or geographical matter about which she happened to express an opinion. His own furies and disappointments, conversely, met only with her sympathetic assent, and she found that when she opened her mouth in public it was her husband's feelings rather than her own that came out of it. It was not because she was cowed that this happened; rather that in matters of the world she judged herself to be her husband's inferior in both intelligence and information. She said things to him in the genuine hope that he might tell her why they were so, as a pupil might ask a question of a teacher. Her ignorance caused her pain, for it really did strike her as sad that the countryside had been despoiled, and she craved an explanation that would make this sadness go away.

'People need room for their businesses,' Mr Daley responded, and Mrs Daley was relieved, almost, of her feelings, the residue of which lingered in her and mingled with her suspicion that her husband found her remarks irritating.

'I'm longing to see that baby,' she said, as the density of the roadside began to suggest to her that they were nearing London. There was a wistful quality to her statement, which she made with no particular expectation of a reply. She did long to see the baby, but it was a strange longing, a longing for the impossible. Unclean forces arrayed themselves around the baby in much the same way as the filthy reaches of London did. Mrs Daley had a desire, which when the baby was older might become a plan, to pluck the child from her unsavoury setting, to convert her back to what was proper and good and right if it wasn't, as by then it might be, too late. 'What a place to be born,' she added, sighing, as they entered the sooty bowels of an underpass.

'Go easy,' Mr Daley unexpectedly asserted, his large body striped like that of a tiger with the tunnel's electric light, 'on Josephine.'

Mrs Daley opened her mouth to reply but nothing came out. She journeyed in offended silence, wincing occasionally as her back gave a twinge. It appeared that the world, all of a sudden, was against her. This atmosphere, of reverses, of slander, of unfair accusation, told her better than any road map that they were approaching Josephine's house: it emanated from her daughter like a strong smell, like a force that could turn things upside down. The traffic, as Mr Daley presently remarked, was good. Soon they were driving in grey, littered streets that Mrs Daley could only distinguish from other grey, littered streets by the fact that she vaguely recognised them. Mr Daley turned the car into Josephine and Roger's road, and drove straight past their house to the other end.

'What are you doing?' she cried out, thinking that some new drama had begun when she had hardly prepared herself for the first, the original drama.

'I'm waiting for a space right outside,' said Mr Daley, turning the car around, 'so that I can see the car from the house.'

They drove up and down the road for ten minutes, Josephine's front door flashing again and again before Mrs Daley's eyes.

'Can't you let me out?' she pleaded finally. 'I'm longing to see the baby.'

At that moment an appropriate space appeared and Mr Daley parked the car in it. They got out and he walked all the way around the car in a manner that reminded Mrs Daley disconcertingly of the behaviour of a dog. They rang the bell and presently Josephine herself opened the door, with the white bundle of the baby in her arms. She cried out at the sight of them and rushed forward to put a fervent arm around her mother's neck in embrace.

'Careful,' trilled Mrs Daley nervously.

'Do you want to hold her?' said Josephine, gesturing with the bundle.

'Let's just wait until we've got inside, shall we?' said Mrs Daley.

'Is my car safe out there?' said Mr Daley, lingering on the doorstep so that nobody heard him except his wife, who didn't care whether the car was safe or not. How could he think about his car, when there was new life afoot? She followed the bundle down the hall and into the sitting room. Roger's house was large, but, as Mrs Daley had often pointed out to Josephine, didn't make use of the space it had. The downstairs was one enormous room, with canvases stacked against the walls and strange pieces of material thrown over the sofa and chairs. The kitchen was tiny and smelled of gas and old food and was not, Mrs Daley suspected, entirely clean. It had no units: everything was kept higgledy-piggledy on shelves, where it gathered a particularly sticky kind of dust. The garden was really just a few paving slabs, on the other side of which stood Roger's studio. He had bought the house, he had explained to Mrs Daley, for the studio, and Mrs Daley had kept to herself – or nearly, anyway – her opinion that, if you had two small children, a garden might have been of more use, and would certainly have been more attractive. She had knocked that studio down, in her mind, several times, and replaced it with a verdant stretch upon which those children, who had been through so much, might play. Now, with the new bundle of white in it, the house seemed to Mrs Daley frankly unacceptable. She cast glances at her husband to ascertain whether he had formed the same opinion, but Mr Daley had sprung up from his place beside her on the sagging sofa and was craning at the front window in order to observe his car.

'Well!' she said sociably. 'This all looks much the same. Where are the children?'

'With Raine,' said Josephine. 'She's bringing them back later.'

Raine was the name of Roger's ex-wife: Mrs Daley had been able to establish no other for her, and because she couldn't bring herself to say it was forced in any conversation that approached the topic to confine herself to sentences in which Raine could be identified by the label 'she'. Mrs Daley felt vaguely disapproving of the idea of the children seeing their mother. It all seemed neither one thing nor the other.

'Is she living in London now?' she enquired.

'I think,' said Josephine, 'she's just here for the weekend. Do you want to hold her?' she added, gesturing again with the bundle.

'In my experience,' said Mrs Daley, 'babies need a little bit of time to get used to new people. They don't like to be hurried.'

'Oh, she loves new people,' Josephine exclaimed.

After just over a week, Mrs Daley didn't see how Josephine could have ascertained this fact; but she drew from it the inference that the house had been full of people and the baby handed around them like a parcel.

'And where is Roger?'

'Working,' said Josephine. 'But he'll come in for lunch.'

At that last word, which exerted a magnetism on him, Mrs Daley had observed, comparable only to that of his car, Mr Daley withdrew from the window and returned to the sofa.

'Can I?' he said, holding out his arms, into which, to Mrs Daley's astonishment, Josephine placed the baby. 'Has she got a name yet?' he robustly enquired.

This was a matter that had been causing Mrs Daley considerable distress. In her kitchen in Ravenley she had pondered it, and with every passing day it appeared to her more and more in the nature of a sacrilege that the baby remained unnamed. The problem was that Mrs Daley knew that the name, when chosen, would displease her, and so during those days she had existed with regard to this question in that strange realm of the impossible, in that exquisite pain of unfulfilment that only Josephine knew how to cause her.

'We think,' said Josephine, 'that she's called Juno.'

The blow was struck, with the added force of its phrasing.

'Hello, Juno,' said Mr Daley, idiotically.

'That's a strange name,' said Mrs Daley in a strangled voice. She wished she were holding the baby now; the time for her intervention had come. Its little movements and noises were close but not close enough. She held out her arms for it but Mr Daley did not yield, so she was driven to lean bodily across him to address the bundle on his lap. 'We think that's a very strange name, don't we, little one?'

'I suppose it is quite strange,' said Josephine. 'But I think it suits her.'

Mrs Daley gave a short laugh.

'The idea of something suiting,' she said, 'a week-old baby!'

'Well,' said Josephine, 'you know what I mean.'

Mrs Daley did not. 'Can I have her?' she asked her husband. In matters concerning children Mrs Daley expected her husband to bow to her, as she did to him in everything else. He surrendered the bundle, as if it were an extravagant hope that he was not surprised to see dashed. With the baby in her arms Mrs Daley felt tears spring to her eyes. 'Poor little thing,' she murmured. The feel of new life! The little arms scything nothingness; the strange tremors and bleatings, the small, wet, gaping mouth; at least Josephine had clothed her in white garments which appeared to be clean. Mrs Daley was reminded, holding the baby, of the almost ugly rawness of the newborn, their half-repellent squirming blindness.

'What's that in her hair?' she enquired, dramatically, of Josephine, for she had discerned dark, matted patches on the baby's downy scalp.

'Blood,' said Josephine bluntly, 'from the birth.'

'Well, haven't you washed her hair?' cried Mrs Daley.

'No,' said Josephine. 'We haven't bathed her yet. You're supposed to wait until the cord drops off. And it's bad for their skin. Don't worry,' she said, 'it won't do her any harm.'

'But babies love their bath!' said Mrs Daley. 'You can't take that away from her!'

The idea that substances from childbirth, that event that posed the chief threat to a belief in a baby's fundamental innocence, could linger unpurged on her skin disturbed and disgusted Mrs Daley. Frequent immersions in soapy water were the way to establish a new life firmly in a blameless realm, far from the acts that had brought it into being.

'Won't you let me wash her?' she said.

'No, Mum,' said Josephine gently.

'Please,' she begged. 'Please just let me take her upstairs. It won't take a moment. You can't,' she stated, meeting Josephine's eyes, 'let her go about with blood in her hair.'

'We'll do it as soon as the cord drops off,' said Josephine. 'The midwife said.'

Mrs Daley took this as a personal affront.

'I've had three children,' she said, 'and I've never heard such nonsense in my life.'

There was a clatter at the back door and the dark figure of Roger loomed up in the glass. Looking at him, Mrs Daley could not for a moment remember whether he was friend or foe, and then recalled that this question remained un-decided. Her husband heaved himself to his feet but she stayed where she was, with the baby on her lap, feeling somewhat hemmed in. Roger always wore jeans, even though he was at least forty; he was wearing them now, with a shirt covered in blotches of paint. Mrs Daley had noted before the narrowness of his hips in those jeans and the contrasting girth of his shoulders. He had large hands that Mrs Daley privately thought of as beautiful, even though it seemed a strange thing to think about hands. It was, she often thought, again privately, such a pity that Roger's connection to their family was so unsatisfactory, so unconventional; she would like to have had him pinned down, trapped in the position of deference towards herself that she understood to be part and parcel of the usual son-in-law relationship. It was unclear to Mrs Daley what exactly she would have done with him, had he been so trapped; but his age, his previous marriage and children, his unwed status with regard to Josephine and something else, something she couldn't put her finger on, guaranteed his freedom and caused her occasionally to feel fear. She wondered if Josephine ever felt this fear, and obscurely rather hoped that she did. She wished she could stand – sitting down, her vanity informed her, she was at a disadvantage. He bent over and kissed her cheek and a lock of his dark hair fell heavily against her forehead.

'What do you think of her?' he said, stroking the baby's face with a finger that had blue paint on it.

'Well!' said Mrs Daley, enthusiastically but non-committally.

'We've already diagnosed an artistic nature,' he said. 'She responds positively to opera, and can tell the difference between Verdi and Wagner.'

'Babies love music,' affirmed Mrs Daley, who did not appear to find such pronouncements ridiculous when Roger made them, although she was unbudging in her view that a week-old baby could not be attributed with a personality. 'Do you want her?' she said finally, making to give him the baby, who she sensed was about to cry.

'I do,' said Roger. 'I've been thinking of her all morning. Unless Josephine wants to feed her – Jo, are you going to feed her?'

'Yes,' said Josephine, sitting down on the sofa next to Mrs Daley.'

Roger withdrew to the kitchen and returned with a bottle of wine.

'The idea,' said Mrs Daley loudly, so that he could hear her, 'of your father knowing whether any of you should be fed or when!'

She was about to continue in this spirit, but was arrested by the sight of Josephine undoing the buttons of her shirt next to her on the sofa.

'Are you feeding her yourself?' she said, alarmed, as Josephine's large, veined breast hove into public view.

'Yes,' said Josephine.

'Wouldn't you prefer,' Mrs Daley continued, lowering her voice to indicate the forsaken concept of discretion, 'to do it somewhere more private?'

'No,' said Josephine. 'Why, does it bother you?'

'I just thought you might be more – *comfortable*, somewhere else.'

Roger handed her a glass of wine and as she looked up she saw her husband standing in front of the fireplace with the white room behind him, and it struck her as strange that he should be there, bodily, when so much of the time his existence seemed to be something that occurred in her own mind, that governed her unseen. He was like a landmark at which, because she lived right next to it, she rarely looked. He had not always been a landmark: once he had moved and breathed, had been separate from her, but over the years this animation had been lifted from within him and transposed to her own inner world, grafted there by a thousand capillaries and threads. She could tell these twin sensibilities apart from one another, but sometimes they confused her.

'It's Josephine's house,' said her husband now. 'She can do what she wants.'

'Thank you, Dad,' said Josephine quietly.

'I just thought,' Mrs Daley cried, 'that she might want some privacy!'

'It's perfectly natural,' pronounced Mr Daley.

'That's not what you said when ours were babies,' she retorted. Blood had surged to her face. 'You forbade me – you said you wouldn't have it!'

'Why would I have said that?' said Mr Daley, more uncertainly. 'Anyway, I couldn't have stopped you. You could have done what you liked.'

'That's not what you said,' Mrs Daley repeated, 'at the time!'

Mr Daley was silent. His face wore an expression of pain. She had never, in thirty-two years, known him to rise up against her so, or she didn't think she had. He gave the appearance of having been converted, mysteriously, to an entirely new set of beliefs. Mrs Daley could win any battle waged on the grounds of memory: her version of the past had long since been accepted between them as the authorised text, and in any case she knew that he couldn't remember that much about it, the past, partly because he hadn't paid enough attention and partly because he had heard her describe things so many times that the original incident had usually got mislaid among the copies. She wondered now whether somehow this original had fallen into his hands. The truth was that she herself couldn't remember exactly what had happened; things came to her down the years not in clear images but in wafts of familiar emotion. These wafts could be more potent than the events themselves, for they hinted at the tragically solitary nature of human feeling: details fell away; other people dissolved and vanished; the minutes before and the minutes after span off into the ether; and Mrs Daley was left alone with the resentments of thirty years before, still as fresh as the day upon which she had felt them.

'How are the children?' she asked Roger, ceremoniously cutting the silence which had gathered in the shabby room. She did not listen, however, to his reply, and so when Mr Daley began to speak again she found that she was not ready for him.

'I must say I admire you,' he said, apparently not to her. 'I can't imagine how difficult it must have been, keeping the family together. People of our generation have very little understanding of a situation such as yours.'

'It's very kind of you to say so,' Roger replied. 'It's all to Josephine's credit.'

'I don't agree,' asserted Mrs Daley, 'that people of our generation have no understanding. True, our parents may not have divorced, but family life was no bed of roses, believe me!' She heard her own voice ringing around the large room. Mrs Daley often had a sense, when she spoke, of her triumphant passage through a situation. Her husband did not possess the art of conversation: he thought conversations were things you had to win. 'I hardly ever saw my father as a child. My mother was on her own for weeks at a time, like a lot of women in those days, during the war. She was, in effect, a single parent,' she added, dramatically. She was beginning to feel slightly drunk.

'My mother was evacuated as a child,' said Roger. 'She hardly saw her parents between the ages of four and eight. I agree, I've often thought there were parallels between her experience and Jack and Poppy's.'

'Oh, the evacuees!' Mrs Daley passionately exclaimed. She had been about to say what a nuisance they were. 'And what was,' she said instead, 'your mother's experience?'

'She had a very difficult time,' said Roger. 'The family she lived with were unkind to her. I don't think she ever really recovered from it. She found it very hard, when we were children, to let us manage our own emotions.'

'Oh, that's disastrous!' said Mrs Daley.

'Well, she struggled to overcome it,' said Roger. 'She taught us to express ourselves as a way of helping her. She was a bit of a pioneer really.'

'But what a burden,' said Mrs Daley, 'for you.'

Josephine always talked about Roger's mother, who was a therapist of one sort or another, in glowing terms. Mrs Daley suspected that they glowed because her own faults were used to fuel them.

'Well if that's true,' laughed Roger, 'then she's certainly paying for it now.'

'Rita's been counselling Jake and Poppy,' explained Josephine, who still sat there with her naked breast for all to see, as though it were the most normal thing in the world. 'I think it's really helped them.'

Mrs Daley experienced a violent surge of impatience. Instinctively she sought the familiar form of her husband, her landmark, as if to reassure herself that she was not lost, that her bearings, her sense of what was right, prevailed, but it appeared that he was no longer there.

'Keeping it in the family,' he said now, apparently with the intention of being humorous.

The room was filled with flat grey light. Occasionally a car passed outside the front window and the sound made its way into Mrs Daley's muffled consciousness. She looked at the strange objects which stood around her, the canvases with their little chaoses of paint, some pieces of carved wood that maddeningly suggested shapes without definitely assuming them, a lamp with a crooked shade, a pale rug of a rough, unfinished weave that lay across the floor, and they seemed to form the lineaments of a world suspended in a long moment of malevolent torpor, a pause on the other side of which stood only the prospect of deterioration and decay. Where was the hope, the joy, the promise, whose aura formed the breathable atmosphere of Mrs Daley's life, of the right outcome? She tried to see in the room some trace of herself, of her influence, and could see none: it neither paid her tribute nor offered her admittance. Roger stood up and loomed towards her, bending over her glass with the bottle. His hips were so close she could have reached out and touched them – that would show them, that would wake them up!

In the gloomy blur of afternoon lunch was finally served, and Mrs Daley apprehended the oily dishes full of cold, foreign vegetables and the strange, flat discs of bread and the cheeses, pungent, collapsing, perceptibly breaking down, as though they were revolving around her in space; as though it were her task to grasp each object and re-establish it in gravity before she was free to go back to her world of solid properties, which appeared to her now to exist in colour where this world lived in monochrome. She was keen to be gone before Raine and the children returned. She had run out of magic: her power to transform, to redeem, had ebbed away. She would be trampled underfoot. With the bulwark of her husband gone, Mrs Daley felt a vertiginous sense of loss. He was in transports now about the food, whose like he claimed never to have eaten in his life. She didn't know how she was going to stop herself from getting up and going to sit outside in the car, among whose controversies at least she felt safe.

'Can I hold her?' she blurted out. Her voice sounded strange; she saw Josephine turn to her with a look of concern. It seemed right that Josephine should be concerned. The baby came to her, as if through the air. Mrs Daley sat there with its faint warmth in her arms. She bent her head and sniffed at the baby's skin. The sour-sweet odour was not one she recognised and she felt a confusing blankness, as if she had been returned to the beginning without knowing why her answer had failed to satisfy.

In the car on the way home, Mr Daley was reserved.

'She seemed quite nice,' said Mrs Daley.

'Who?' said Mr Daley.

'Raine,' Mrs Daley gallantly stammered, pleased to find that she was able to pronounce the word now that she was familiar with the object it represented. 'She's a lovely-looking girl,' she added.

Mrs Daley had the satisfying feeling of having stolen a march on her husband. Roger's ex-wife had turned up, in the littered closing stages of the afternoon, to return the children. Mrs Daley, who had so feared this meeting, found it, to her surprise, painless; more than that, she had discerned in it the possibility of pleasure. The ex-wife – she was, after all, the first, the true wife – seemed to her to represent the necessary, the right and proper devolution of power away from the centre of Josephine. She was like a column of hard fact standing in the fog of relativity, of all that dreary talk of difficulties and counselling, of Mr Daley's pathetic enthusiasms and her own perpetual exile from the warm, conniving heart of her daughter's existence – here, at last, was someone she could get along with! The unorthodoxy of the connection gratified Mrs Daley's dramatic sense. She had enjoyed, too, the experience of finding Josephine out: the body, the evidence, stood before her. She had exchanged pleasantries, and more, with this body, which was small and slim and fair-haired and which added, she thought, a much needed dash of adventure to the proceedings.

'Didn't you think?' she probed, as her husband had not replied.

'I didn't,' he said, 'notice.'

'I wonder,' wondered Mrs Daley, aloud, 'what went wrong between her and Roger. They must have made the most striking couple! It's terribly sad. I do hope,' she added cautiously, 'that Josephine wasn't naughty. Especially not with children involved. I must say, *I* wouldn't like to have a glamorous first wife hanging around. Particularly not with a new baby – one's hardly at one's most attractive!'

Mr Daley drove resolutely on. Really, thought Mrs Daley, he paid so little attention to her that she could have said what she liked.

But she could not; she was not as free of obligations as she sometimes, pondering the ingratitude with which her family wore the fact of their biological debt to her, felt herself to be.

Barely two weeks after their visit to London, her husband informed her that Josephine had telephoned to say that she and the baby were coming to stay. Mrs Daley had been out at the time: had she been at home, she would not have capitulated to this request as her husband had done. She had no appetite for Josephine; she remained sated by the lunch she had been served in the untidy house. Besides, it was December, the month of Christmas and of the Daleys' annual drinks party. Mrs Daley liked to give these two events a wide berth – they represented a change from her usual diet of concerns. Josephine, being everyday fare, she viewed as an obstacle to this pleasure. Nevertheless her daughter had arrived, steadily, like a contagion sweeping south, and had taken a grip on the spare room, where for the past five days she had existed in gloomy disarray, lying in bed until all hours and hardly bothering to tidy up the baby's things. Mrs Daley had penetrated this fastness only once, by persuading Josephine to take a bath, and had discovered in her absence that the bed sheets were covered with large yellow stains. Alarmed, she had been unable for a moment to think of what these stains could signify. It finally occurred to her that they were milk stains; in their way, as disgusting as the other kind, for Josephine slept with the baby in her bed and wouldn't hear of her having a proper cot of her own. There were dirty nappies in the wastepaper bin, and T-shirts with tidemarks around the chest strewn all over the place.

But today Josephine had descended to the kitchen, and installing herself at the table with the baby on her lap and her shirt unbuttoned, had promptly asked her mother whether she ever thought of getting rid of the house.

'I have lived in this house for nearly twenty-eight years,' said Mrs Daley, 'and I shall die here!'

Mrs Daley had made this pronouncement before, or a version of it – the number changed, in spite of the exactitude of that 'nearly'. Her occupation of her house was a grand, a mythic thing.

'I just thought,' said Josephine, 'that it might be getting on top of you. It seems like a lot of space for two people.'

'Two people!' replied Mrs Daley, with incredulity. 'Would that it were! There's hardly been a weekend this year when one or other of you hasn't been down, wanting some fresh air and some home-cooked food! I should put up a sign outside – Hotel, no vacancies!'

Mrs Daley remembered another house, a small, modern redbrick house on the south coast, or near enough. She had been reminded of this house only recently. Josephine had got out the family photograph albums, wanting to see pictures of herself as a baby, and Mrs Daley had been surprised to be confronted by irrefutable evidence not only that she had, at one time, lived in that house but that her children had lived there too. She had said so many times that she had borne and brought up her children in Ravenley that she was sincerely startled to discover that she hadn't.

'I could never go back,' she said now, 'to those days in Boxborough, when there were three of you in one room. The bath was in the kitchen! I used to have to go out and sit on the doorstep if I wanted to have a cup of tea in peace.'

'I don't know how you managed,' said Josephine.

'Oh, they were happy days!' Mrs Daley assured her. 'I sometimes think now,' she said wistfully, 'that those days in Boxborough were the happiest of my life. To have one of those days again!'

'What was it about them,' said Josephine, 'that made them so happy?'

Mrs Daley was unused to being called so directly to account. People rarely asked her how she felt or what she thought.

'I don't know,' she said now. She grasped and grasped. 'We didn't have much,' she began. 'And now we have such a lot.'

'And yet it was then that you were happy,' said Josephine. 'But at the same time you say that you could never go back.'

'Oh, you can never go back,' said Mrs Daley. She felt that perhaps she wouldn't say anything else.

'I know what you mean,' said Josephine. 'When I think about the past I feel almost bereaved. I feel that the person I was then is dead, and that all I want is to see that person again, if only, like you say, for a day.'

'I'm not sure,' said Mrs Daley, 'that I feel that exactly. All I know is that for all the happiness we had at Boxborough, I couldn't go back to living in a smaller house.'

Josephine, since her arrival, certainly seemed to want to talk, particularly about the past. Mrs Daley had no concrete objection to talking about the past, other than that it un-settled her slightly. The past was a place in which she loomed larger than she did today. She liked to look at it vaguely, from a distance, where it formed a pleasant vista of her own importance. Close up its component parts became more evident; its detail oppressed her: she received an impression of her culpability that reminded her of the more tiresome aspects of being responsible for a house, three children and a husband.

'Did you want to have children?' Josephine enquired.

'Of course!' said Mrs Daley. What a question! This was the fashion now, to ask questions about the most basic things, as if one had any choice in the matter. She didn't object to following fashion, though, particularly when it concerned things that happened so long ago that it made no difference what you said about them. 'There wasn't anything else I could have done,' she added.

'But did you actually want to?'

'Well.' Mrs Daley considered. 'That was just what you did, in those days.'

'I never wanted to,' said Josephine.

Mrs Daley, who had decided early and irrevocably that Josephine's visit was entirely normal, and subsequently that it was not only normal but as imperative as the seasons that a new mother should spend a period – the figure Mrs Daley had grasped from the air was two weeks – with her own mother, now wondered whether Josephine's behaviour was an established aspect of this tradition.

'I'm sure you did,' she ventured. It surely did not require pointing out that whatever Josephine had thought about having children in the past, it was now too late to change her mind. 'It's a good thing our bodies don't always obey our minds,' she added.

'Sometimes I look at her,' said Josephine slowly, 'and I think, What have I done?'

'It's entirely natural,' said Mrs Daley, 'for a new mother to have a period of mourning.'

She didn't know where this phrase had come from. It had seemed to come from the kettle, which had long since boiled and was now emitting a faint plume of steam.

'Is it?' said Josephine.

'Well – yes,' said Mrs Daley. 'Everything seems upside down for a while. I remember weeping buckets after I had Christopher! Your father would come home at the end of the day and find me still in bed crying my eyes out.'

'That's awful,' said Josephine.

'All he cared about was his dinner,' said Mrs Daley, laughing bitterly. 'He used to go round the house looking for it and when he didn't find it he would threaten to send me back to my parents!'

'I can't believe it,' said Josephine, shaking her head.

Mrs Daley, satisfied that she had given Josephine something to chew on, got up to make coffee. She was hoping to get Josephine and the baby out of the house by eleven o'clock. Mrs Walcott was coming to clean.

'Why have you never told me that before?' demanded Josephine.

'You never asked,' sniffed Mrs Daley.

'I never thought about it,' said Josephine wonderingly. 'I never thought about your life before you had me.'

'Oh, I had plenty of life,' said Mrs Daley with a short laugh.

'Do you ever talk about it now, with Dad?'

'Talk about what?'

'About the crying.'

'Your father doesn't like talking about the past. He probably wouldn't even remember,' said Mrs Daley.

'How did you forgive him?' said Josephine. 'Did you still love him?'

'Well, I'm still here, thirty years later,' said Mrs Daley. 'Marriage isn't like that,' she added, as this statement sounded rather flat. 'You have your ups and downs, but you don't just throw it all away because of what one of you does on a particular day. You can't be selfish, in a marriage. I'm not saying it isn't difficult. But if something's worthwhile then you stick with it, through the bad times as well as the good.'

Having delivered this gritty speech, Mrs Daley was surprised to notice that Josephine had laid her head down on the kitchen table and was crying. She glanced at the clock and saw that it was ten to eleven. Mrs Daley's hospitality, after five days of having Josephine and the baby in the house, was at a low ebb. She needed Mrs Walcott to cleanse her system. She needed to erase, in order to begin again.

'Why don't you put the baby in the pram,' she said, 'and take her out for a nice walk. It'll make you feel much better.'

Mrs Daley had had the foresight to borrow a pram from Vanessa Healey down in the village before Josephine's arrival, with the idea of making the occasional picturesque promenade in the lane should the right moment suggest itself. This arrangement had proved to be more practical than she had quite meant it to be: Josephine had arrived without any equipment for the baby at all, and Vanessa Healey's pram, which Mrs Daley had found in the event to be too old-fashioned and not very clean and had therefore tactfully wheeled into the garage, had since been wheeled out again.

'I'm so tired,' wept Josephine, without raising her head. 'I'm just so tired.'

'You'll feel better once you've had a walk. I've got Mrs Walcott coming in five minutes,' she said finally, when it seemed that Josephine was not going to move. 'You probably don't want her to see you upset.'

Once Josephine had gone, and the sound of the hoover upstairs and the smells of bleach and polish were drifting reliably over Mrs Daley in soothing waves, she went out to the garden in search of her husband. Mrs Daley rarely entered her garden. At the front of the house there were beds and a gravelled circle where visitors parked their cars, and Mrs Daley occasionally pottered about out there when the weather was nice and she liked the picture she made, in her sunhat and gloves; if anyone arrived, she was pleased for them to find her thus. The back garden, with its large square of lawn, its cyprus trees, its anomalous plants and bushes, was more foreign terrain: it was where Mr Daley kept his shed, and had taken on in Mrs Daley's eyes a masculine flavour, an inelegant boldness, a plain and stolid aspect. Mr Daley's shed was a small wooden pavilion that stood on the far corner of the lawn beside an overgrown laurel. He had bought it on his retirement and now kept office hours there. Mrs Daley thought this was a sensible arrangement. She and her husband had seemed tacitly to agree that, having never been in the house during the day before, it would be curious for him suddenly to start. Their lives had evolved in a regulated climate: their marital day was short. They did not exist in relation to each other between nine and five – during those hours they were strangers. Mrs Daley had feared losing the privacy of this estrangement, which fuelled like a lung the outlying intimacy. But her husband was decisive, he was proud: he too, it seemed, had secrets. In his shed he smoked cigars and listened to the radio and did crosswords and lately, she gathered from her occasional incursions there, had started reading, long books with inscrutable covers that he put down when her face appeared in the glass, and which left him with a lingering expression that was unfamiliar to Mrs Daley. It was understood that she should not harry him in his shed. It was a point of honour. There he was, like a rat in a trap, his dignity exposed – it was required that she leave him alone. Unless it was important, of course; the burden of proof in this matter rested on Mrs Daley, as it had when she used to telephone him at work.

He would often ask if she had called him just to tell him what she had just told him. She didn't care whether she had or not, although she never said so.

'I've just had Josephine,' she dramatically informed him now, 'crying in the kitchen!'

Mr Daley put down his book. The shed was cold. The tang of cigar smoke assailed Mrs Daley's nostrils. Everything seemed brown. This was what men were, without women.

'Did you upset her?' said Mr Daley, warningly.

'She upset herself,' said Mrs Daley. 'We were talking about this and that, and she just broke down. I sent her out for a nice walk with the pram. I'm sure she'll be fine.'

Mrs Daley felt a need to return to the house. Her husband did not function well as a channel for news. He absorbed things without giving back the faintest echo, but he also gave her the impression that when she told him something, he heard something completely different. The telephone, the telephone was what she wanted. She had made a mistake. She needed to put herself in reverse.

'You should go after her,' said Mr Daley, 'and make sure she's all right.'

'Why wouldn't she be all right? She's quite safe in Ravenley.'

'Josephine is under a lot of strain. She needs to be helped.'

'She's absolutely fine,' said Mrs Daley irritably. 'She's just like any other mother with a new baby. What sort of strain could she possibly be under? She's got one tiny baby and everyone falling over themselves to help her. I never had anyone worrying that I was under strain, or making sure that I was all right!'

To her surprise Mrs Daley felt tears spring to her own eyes. It was too pitiful! Was it true? She strained to remember. It had to be true – where would she have got it from otherwise?

'You were different,' stated Mr Daley.

'In what way was I different?' demanded Mrs Daley.

'You were stronger,' said Mr Daley presently.

Mrs Daley was rendered temporarily speechless by this observation. Her husband rose to his feet.

'Where are you going?' she cried.

'To see if I can find her,' he replied.

She ran after him across the lawn, not wishing to be left alone in his lair. In the hall she found Mrs Walcott, dusting the picture frames.

'Oh, Mrs Walcott!' she exclaimed, as she saw the front door close behind her husband. 'We're terribly worried about Josephine! She's gone off with the baby in the most dreadful state! My husband's gone after her – oh, I do hope she's all right!'

She had a vague impression of Mrs Walcott's soft, white, anxious face. There seemed to be no reason that she could think of why household familiars shouldn't know about their family ups and downs. It was all part of the human drama; it was part of life. This idea that you had to keep everything private – well, what for? What did any of them have to hide? Mr Daley returned after some time, with Josephine. She looked pale but in no particular distress. Mr Daley asserted repeatedly that she was cold, and went off to the sitting room to light a fire.

'Why didn't you take a coat?' said Mrs Daley.

'I forgot,' said Josephine. 'Would you mind having her for a bit?'

She offered the baby, clad in a brightly coloured padded outfit, to Mrs Daley, who opened her mouth to say that in fact she had rather a lot of things to do and then closed it again. Although she hadn't said it outright to Josephine, she had been observing something of a stand-off in the matter of looking after the baby. As she had told her friends, over the telephone, out of earshot, you couldn't be expected to look after a baby if you couldn't give it its milk; they had agreed that it was difficult. Mrs Daley had considered, before Josephine's arrival, taking things into her own hands. To this end she had purchased feeding bottles and a tin of formula milk, and stood them on a high shelf in one of the kitchen cupboards, with ambivalent feelings about the prospect of their discovery. As it was, she hadn't had much to do with the baby at all. She hadn't really bonded with it, she told her friends. It seemed like a very clingy baby; it wanted to be with its mother, a stance that was both right and relieving and for which Mrs Daley at the same time reproached it, for she already had five grandchildren, none of whom seemed to mind being with her at all and might even have preferred it to being with their own parents, had they been impolite enough to express an opinion. With her experience, she could tell when a baby didn't like her, even if it was only four weeks old. This one had already got its own way too many times for Mrs Daley's taste. She took the baby into the kitchen and removed its outer layer. It regarded her with bright, suspicious eyes. She was startled by the sight of its small, bony body, its wrinkled purple hands, the preternatural torsion of its legs, its bald, outsized skull. It wrinkled in her arms and made tiny sneezing noises. Its tongue, sharp, curled, emerged from its mouth and probed the air, and the quavering siren of its cry uncoiled after it. She immediately went in search of Josephine, but was blockaded at the sitting-room door by her husband.

'The baby's hungry,' said Mrs Daley.

'Josephine's asleep,' said Mr Daley, 'on the sofa. I put a blanket over her.'

'Well, I'm afraid she'll have to wake up,' said Mrs Daley.

'Can't you give her something to eat?' said Mr Daley, and Mrs Daley snorted with triumphant delight.

'The idea,' she said, 'of giving food to a four-week-old baby!'

The truth was that she couldn't remember exactly when babies started to eat food, but she didn't think it was at four weeks old.

'Well, she'll have to cry,' said Mr Daley grimly. 'It won't do her any harm. We'll wake Josephine at –' he consulted his watch '– three o'clock. Try and keep her out of earshot until then.'

Mrs Daley returned to the kitchen. The clock stood at one-thirty. Mrs Walcott was upstairs, doing the beds. At any moment, she would discover Josephine's stained sheets. The baby's crying had reached a pitch where it resembled silence: it filled the kitchen like water; it formed an element in which Mrs Daley's mind bobbed about, now submerged, now surfacing. She lifted the baby upright and placed it against her shoulder. Its body objected stiffly. Mrs Daley began to pace. A little tune suggested itself to her. She hummed it, and paced along in time. After two circuits of the kitchen table, the level of sound seemed to drop. The body yielded slightly. Mrs Daley circled a few more times and then decided to change her route, describing instead two sides of a square along the kitchen cabinets. The level rose; she resumed her circular formation. The baby felt thin and bony against her shoulder – she'd always suspected they didn't get enough, being fed that way! – and so passing a drawer she deftly withdrew from it a handful of clean tea-towels and padded the baby's back with them. Presently, the crying ceased. Mrs Daley continued to pace; she wasn't out of the woods yet. After a while she stopped and, swaying from foot to foot, craned her head to look at the baby's face. It was resting on her shoulder with its eyes shut. Its eyelids were thin and blue. Its tiny, chiselled features were still.

With the warm clamp of it on her shoulder she slowly eased herself into a chair. Strange feelings were climbing, like vines, through her body. It unsettled her to be holding Josephine's baby in this intimate clasp: it was as if she were holding Josephine herself. She had not held Josephine much as a baby, or even touched her. She hadn't done right by her. She had known it at the time and she knew it still, for she had never undone it, though she had meant to. Every day on which she had failed to rectify it had seemed to guarantee the next, and the next, until this wrongdoing was years old, until she hated Josephine, having missed the opportunity to love her. Unwatched, alone at home with her children, she had played with Christopher while Josephine cried in her cot in another room. Josephine had seemed to her an aberration: some dark doubt in Mrs Daley had expressed itself in her flesh; and so Mrs Daley, too, was aberrant, she treated her badly, and Josephine had appeared to understand this darkness, to be a part of it. It was a form of self-loathing; it was in some ways a game, because what else did she have to do, how else could she express herself, when she hardly spoke to another adult, when she did nothing but clean and cook and look after children all day? And now that Josephine was grown, this game, in which love was withheld, was something they played together. Very occasionally, Mrs Daley felt that she might soon surrender, but more often Josephine made her bellicose, except it was a strange aggression, in that she hoped by it to make Josephine hurt her, and to feel as a result that she was not her tormentor but her victim.

The baby stirred in its sleep and began to gnaw her shoulder. The clock said two. Her husband, as far as she knew, continued to guard the sitting room door. Mrs Daley patted the baby and hummed a little. How could anyone, seeing her now, say that she was bad? She had broken Josephine as she might, visiting the house of someone she didn't know well, have broken a precious piece of china: by accident and unobserved, and being too ashamed to confess it she had swept up the fragments and hidden them. Sometimes in her feelings for her daughter she caught sight of this secret truth as if she hadn't known it was there; and the sight gave her a fresh impression of her own innocence to add to the greater story, to the conviction she had formed, over the years, that in this matter she had been unlucky, that she was to be pitied not blamed, that if anyone was damaged, broken, under strain, it was she herself. Mrs Daley tightened her hold. She and this little baby, alone in the world, unloved!

'Now we're for it,' she said to the baby, as its head thumped impotently on her shoulder. It was gnawing at its fist – it was starving! 'Why don't we see what grandma's got for you?' she said, rising to her feet.

It was funny how you didn't forget: she held the baby with one arm and made the bottle with the other as though she were recalling the much-practised steps of an old dance. She put in an extra scoop or two of powder for good measure. The baby drank it down, every last drop. Mrs Daley felt that they had negotiated a tricky junction and were now on the open road. She didn't see what this baby was going to do without her. It was time for her to sleep now, now that she was satisfied. Mrs Daley felt sure that she would sleep for a long time. As she didn't have a cot, Mrs Daley was forced in the end to make a bed for her out of tea-towels in the dirty old pram Vanessa Healey had lent her, which she wheeled in and stood on newspapers in the kitchen. While the baby slept Mrs Daley could give it a good clean.

The invitations were all posted, except the Porters', which Mrs Daley thought she would deliver by hand. She had never been inside the Porters' house, a great pink thing next to the church; nor had anyone else in the village, as far as she knew. They were not much seen but they were greatly talked of. The talk was mostly of her, of course, with her name in the newspapers every week. Mrs Daley didn't believe that half as many people had read her column as spoke about it in the most extravagent terms. She had bought the newspaper herself once or twice, but it always seemed to be the wrong day.

She put on her camel-hair coat and her navy court shoes and decided to drive, even though it was only down the lane, but the Porters' front garden was wet and overgrown and she could find no path to the door so her shoes were ruined in any case. She knocked and presently Serena appeared. She was dressed entirely in black and her red hair hung loose around her face. The colour, which now that she was close to it Mrs Daley could see was voluntary, was certainly dramatic, though rather unkind to her pale complexion. She regarded Mrs Daley with the wide, unblinking gaze of a cat. Mrs Daley had not, in the strictest sense, met Serena before, but she had seen her often, driving fast up the lane past Hill House with two small children strapped in the back of the car and looking out of the window, as it seemed to Mrs Daley, forlornly.

'I've been meaning to come down and see how you were settling in,' she said, 'but you know how it is – busy lives!'

She laughed gaily and the shadow of her laugh passed over Serena's crooked mouth.

'I'm a great fan of your column,' continued Mrs Daley. She wondered, suddenly, whether she had lipstick on her teeth.

'Come in,' said Serena.

'I won't keep you long,' said Mrs Daley, following her through the hall and into the kitchen. 'I can't bear it when people just *present* themselves, can you? The telephone's been the most marvellous invention in that respect – it's far easier to get rid of people when they can't see what you're doing. I spend my *life* on the telephone! It drives my husband completely mad – he says it's like living with a lunatic, because he only gets to hear one side of the conversation. I think men simply don't feel the same need to communicate, do they?'

'Probably not,' said Serena, contemplatively.

'What *do* you think men talk about, when they're together?' said Mrs Daley. Serena struck her as thin and rather wan, and the kitchen was a disaster area. Dirty dishes and newspapers were piled everywhere, and the floor was covered with children's toys. 'I must have heard them talk plenty of times, and yet when I try to think of what they say or how they say it I can't remember. I play this little game with my husband sometimes, where I decide not to say anything more and to see how long it will take him to say something, and he always wins. Sometimes I can't even imagine what he *would* say. As far as I know, if I didn't speak we'd spend the rest of our lives in silence! Now that would be a good subject for one of your columns, wouldn't it?' she said, inclining her head, for Serena impressed her as a person who needed help. 'How women keep the whole human conversation going. You could call it something like –' she looked to the ceiling for inspiration '– "Talking to Ourselves"!'

'That's a good idea,' said Serena.

' "Talking to Ourselves",' whispered Mrs Daley. 'Yes, I can think of plenty of people who'd be interested in that. Plenty of women, that is! I always wondered whether my daughter Josephine would be a writer,' she continued. 'She's very emotional – she gets that from me – but she lacks ambition. She always looks on the negative side. There's always a problem with everything. I say to her, You know, you're going to lose all the positive – you're going to drive people away. Nothing is perfect!'

'No,' said Serena.

'Nothing is perfect,' reiterated Mrs Daley. 'I think that all this women's lib has given girls today the most impossible expectations. They want everything, and when they get it they don't know what to do with it because it isn't perfect. But men *aren't* perfect. Children *aren't* perfect. They don't always fit in with your plans. My daughter is always saying to me, Mum, how did you do it? And I say, We simply didn't think about it. We accepted our lot and tried to look on the bright side. We didn't expect anybody to thank us, but we didn't complain about it either. I remember,' she continued thoughtfully, 'when I was pregnant with my first child, there was a girl living nearby who I used to see quite a lot of. She already had two children, and I thought we might be friends. But I never saw this girl without her complaining, about what hard work it all was, about how unfair it was, how difficult she found it being at home with the children – poor little mites! – how her husband didn't understand, how she was depressed and goodness knows what. In the end I made a decision. I thought, Why should I let this girl spoil everything for me? And do you know what I did? I simply stopped going there, and if she came to my house I pretended I wasn't at home. I didn't want this girl around when my baby came into the world. Later I found out that everyone else had thought the same thing. This girl didn't have a friend left!'

Just then a man whom Mrs Daley knew must be Victor Porter, although he didn't look like the Victor Porter she had imagined, came into the kitchen with the two children she had seen through the windows of Serena's car.

'This is my husband,' said Serena. 'And this is – I'm sorry, I've forgotten your name.'

'Barbara Daley,' said Mrs Daley. 'I was just telling your wife what great fans we all are around here! She's quite the talk of the town – metaphorically speaking!'

'How do you do,' said Victor Porter. He did not say anything else. He was quite unsavoury-looking, she decided. He couldn't have been older than forty-three or so, but he looked like an old man. He was thin and bony and hunched his shoulders, and he seemed to have lost most of his hair.

'And these are the children!' she cried.

The children, and their parents, stared at her in reply with eyes that struck Mrs Daley, as if from afar, as communicating insufficient encouragement for her to extend her stay much longer. It occurred to her to think that she did not entirely like the Porters, but the sentiment was currently so out of vogue that she did not think it. Instead she stored it away for the future, when it may or may not be of use. Fashions changed, after all. In the car on the way home, she realised that she had forgotten to give them their invitation. She took her foot off the accelerator and the car bounced slowly along. She would put it in the post. She pressed the pedal, and sped back up the hill to the house.

'I think,' said Mr Daley, 'that we should call the doctor.'

'I don't see why,' said Mrs Daley. 'It isn't as if she's actually ill.'

'That's for the doctor to decide,' said her husband, who was standing in the middle of the sitting room and making for the door. He was like a fish that kept slipping off its hook; only by speaking again could she reel him back.

'You don't go to the doctor for being unhappy,' she said, with a little laugh that felt as though it might spark a deeper, louder laughter but didn't. 'Can you imagine!'

'Depression is a recognised medical condition,' her husband replied.

That laughter which had never happened was rolling around inside her. Occasionally it rose up into her throat and caused her chest to convulse.

'I think I'd know if Josephine was depressed,' she said. 'She just wants attention – that's all there is to it. It's perfectly normal after having a baby, and I should know. You've spent your whole life being the centre of attention and then suddenly there's this little scrap that everyone's taking more notice of than you – it sounds silly, but believe me, it can be very difficult!'

Her husband had been sidling to the door again during this speech.

'I think you should take the baby up now,' he said, with his hand on the door handle.

'Oh, just a minute longer!' said Mrs Daley, clutching the baby to her chest. She had decided to call her Daisy – in private, of course. 'We're having such a nice time, aren't we, darling?'

'She needs to be with her mother,' said Mr Daley.

'I don't get the impression,' Mrs Daley replied, 'that Josephine would care if she never saw this baby again.'

She met her husband's eye with a challenging look. His hand fell back to his side.

'Don't say that,' he replied.

'Every time I take her in there Josephine starts to cry!'

'She has to see her,' said Mr Daley. 'It's imperative.'

'And what about this little mite? I don't see why she should suffer. Anyway,' she added, 'it's not as if she really needs her. She's quite happy to take her milk from me.'

'The less said about that,' said Mr Daley, 'the better.'

'Well, what did you expect me to do? Let her starve?'

'I don't know,' said Mr Daley, removing his glasses, without which he looked like a great big mole, and rubbing his eyes. 'I just don't know.'

Mr Daley was beginning to say that he didn't know rather too often for Mrs Daley's taste. What didn't he know?

'I don't expect you to thank me,' she said. The little laugh came up again and fluttered frantically in her throat. 'Goodness knows,' she added, 'I've had to learn not to expect thanks. But I do expect you to be on my side. I've got a baby on my hands all day, a house that's upside down and forty people coming for Christmas drinks the day after tomorrow, and if you've got any solutions I'd be glad to hear about them. But please don't treat me as though I've done something wrong, when all I've ever tried to do is what's best for everybody!'

She could not have put it better: all this dreary moralising, this talk of problems, at Christmas! The fact was that for the past thirty years her husband hadn't had the faintest idea of how she'd spent her time, and hadn't seemed to care much, either – she could have been a shoplifter, or a murderer, but as long as she'd had dinner on the table when he came home from work it hadn't mattered what she was.

'Give me the baby,' said Mr Daley, holding out his hands.

'I'll take her up,' said Mrs Daley, 'if you insist. But don't expect me to stay if Josephine causes a scene.'

She rose and left the room. On the stairs she waited to see if he would follow her, but he did not. She trod silently along the thick carpet on the upstairs landing. The door to Josephine's bedroom was shut. The sight of that door – so confidently, aggressively closed! – provoked in Mrs Daley the desire to smash and break. How dared Josephine close that door, which did not belong to her? Mrs Daley flung it open, rattling the handle in the hope of hearing loud noises, but the handle was well fixed and soundless and the carpet thick. Josephine's room was full of a warm, sour smell. The curtains were closed. Her daughter lay in a heap under the bedclothes.

'Wake up!' she commanded, closing the door behind her.

'I am awake,' mumbled Josephine.

Mrs Daley marched across the room and wrenched open the curtains. Josephine did not move.

'I've had enough of this nonsense!' said Mrs Daley shrilly. She had not realised she was going to say this. It seemed that she was extremely angry. It also seemed that had she not been holding Daisy, she would have struck Josephine's prone body. She would have rained blows on her through the bedclothes until she came cowering out from underneath them. 'Now get out of that bed immediately!'

'I can't,' said Josephine.

'Get out!' she cried. 'Get out!'

Mrs Daley lunged towards her daughter and tore the bedclothes back. Josephine lay on her side in a crumpled nightdress. Her body was shaking with sobs. At the sight of this body Mrs Daley's fury left her. She felt frightened. She sat on the edge of the bed and considered the situation.

'I don't know what to do,' she said. 'I'm at my wits'.end.'

It was all very confusing. For a moment she could not remember what was real and what was not. She kept hearing things that she thought people had said, unpleasant things that she must have imagined, so unpleasant were they. And a poor little child being hit as she lay in her bed! She had forgotten all about that! Had it been her? She had certainly been there. Why had she not remembered it before? It might have helped – it might have made all the difference! It was in a room with pink-patterned wallpaper. She felt a tremendous pity for herself, even as she recalled, very fleetingly, that that room had been Josephine's, in the old house, and that it was she, Barbara Daley, who had struck the child again and again through the bedclothes. And yet it did not seem that way; it seemed the other way around. She heard the door open; she felt the blows. What it was to be a mother! It had hurt her, all of it, more than it had hurt them, a thousand times more!

'I think we ought to call Roger,' she said faintly.

'I don't want Roger,' sobbed Josephine. 'I never want to see him again.' She buried her head in her arms and moaned.

'Why ever not?' said Mrs Daley, startled.

'Can't I just stay here with you?' said Josephine; or at least that's what Mrs Daley thought she said; her head remained buried in her arms and her voice was obscured. Mrs Daley regarded her dishevelled body with distaste. Josephine had put on weight. Her skin was plump and smooth and gave off a musky smell. Tangled hanks of dark hair fell over her face. Mrs Daley looked away. The room was in chaos. She placed the baby, who had gone to sleep, at the other end of the bed and banked her in with pillows. Clothes, all of which looked vaguely unclean, lay everywhere – Mrs Daley scooped them up, averting her eyes, and threw them out into the hall. She arranged the bottles and jars on the dresser into neat rows. Wads of tissue paper lay everywhere, and Mrs Daley placed them in the wastepaper bin, avoiding closer inspection. Presently, having straightened everything and wrenched open the window an inch or two, she was compelled to return to the fact of her daughter.

'Let's sit you up, shall we?' she said grimly.

To her surprise, Josephine complied with this instruction quite willingly, so that Mrs Daley had to do no more than lay her fingers on her shoulder. Josephine grasped at these fingers with a hot hand and Mrs Daley withdrew them quickly. She had always suspected that Josephine was lascivious in her relationships with men. She had suspected it ever since Josephine was a little girl. In Roger's house, for example, on her way to the lavatory, Mrs Daley had found lewd sketches for which Josephine had presumably been the model. She could not understand why these sketches had not been better hidden. What sort of atmosphere was that, for young children to live in? Aside from being inappropriate – Josephine's speciality – these sketches had confirmed something that Mrs Daley had always hoped to see denied once her daughter was out in the world, namely that other people found Josephine attractive and that that quality in her which repelled Mrs Daley was invisible to everybody else. She had wanted Josephine to suffer rejection but she hadn't, she had been accepted again and again, and when she rejected these men who claimed to love her Mrs Daley always thought, and often said, that very soon this nasty habit would catch up with her and she would find herself alone. But she never did; there was always someone else. Mrs Daley had wondered whether Roger might buck this trend. He was an artist – everyone knew what they were like. If he sketched Josephine, whom else might he one day want to sketch? Mrs Daley reminded herself that she did not, strictly speaking, wish for her daughter's unhappiness. It was just that she felt that some long lie, a wound of injustice that afflicted her life and never seemed to heal, would be exposed by Josephine being brought to account elsewhere. If it could only be proved that Josephine was difficult, how much easier it would be for Mrs Daley to love her!

'I think we'll give that hair a brush,' she said. Josephine sat there with a brimming face. A large tear rolled out of her eye and down her cheek. 'Daisy's having a lovely sleep!' exclaimed Mrs Daley, conversationally.

'Who?' said Josephine.

'I mean the baby!' cried Mrs Daley. 'What was I thinking of? I always wanted to call you Daisy,' she added, drawing the brush through Josephine's hair, which emitted a dry, dirty smell. 'But your father wouldn't have it. He said it didn't go with Daley. I thought it was such a pretty name for a little girl.'

'What difference would it have made?' said Josephine.

'Oh none, I'm sure!' said Mrs Daley hastily. 'It's just that these things seem to matter so much at the time.'

'All I remember,' said Josephine, 'is feeling as though I'd done something wrong, but never finding out what it was.'

'What on earth do you mean! As a child?'

'It's funny,' said Josephine. 'I always thought that as I got older those things would matter less. But they don't, they matter more. I thought that when I had the baby I would die, because it felt so much like the end of something. It felt like I'd gone around in a big circle and come back to the beginning. But I didn't die.'

'Of course you didn't!' agreed Mrs Daley. 'People don't die in childbirth any more, thank goodness.'

'And yet,' said Josephine, 'here I am. Back at the beginning,' she added, before Mrs Daley had time to ask her where. 'It's almost like I'm a baby again. All I want to do is cry and sleep. Isn't it sad, the way babies cry? It's as though they know something that the rest of us have forgotten.'

'But—'

'And I can't get it out of my head that very soon I'm going to find out.'

'Find out what?'

'I don't know. What's in the dark. Something bad.'

'Josephine,' said Mrs Daley, who didn't like the sound of this, 'I think you really must try to get a grip on yourself.'

To her alarm, Josephine flung herself sideways and put her head in Mrs Daley's lap, encircling her middle with her arms.

'Please,' she sobbed. 'Please don't make me go back!'

Mrs Daley held herself rigid. Her hands were frozen in little postures above Josephine's head. She worried about her skirt, which was new and into which Josephine was mashing her face.

'Is it Roger?' she said. 'Has he done something wrong?'

Josephine turned her head sideways on Mrs Daley's lap. Her arms remained tenaciously locked around her waist.

'I don't want him to take my baby,' she said.

'Well, I don't think there's any chance of that! The baby's right here!'

'He's done it before,' said Josephine. 'He took Raine's babies. He thinks they belong to him. He said she was mad and that's what he'll say about me.'

Mrs Daley looked out of the window in despair, as if to see time visibly passing there, with its cargo of undone tasks. It was snowing. The flakes fell straight down from the flat grey sky. She needed, urgently, to make contact with practical things, to create future events with which to ballast the day. She was beginning to forget who she was – she felt unreeled, like a long piece of thread wound off its spool. The world threatened her with the prospect of its imminent collapse.

'Why don't you come downstairs,' she said, while her face felt as though it would shatter if she had to speak even another word, 'and help me in the kitchen. I've got forty people coming for Christmas drinks the day after tomorrow, and with one thing and another I've got terribly behind.'

And that, shortly afterwards, was how Mr Daley found them, making mince pies together in the kitchen with the baby propped up in her pram – what a picture they made, Mrs Daley thought, if one erased the dark circles under

Josephine's eyes and tidied her up a bit! Yet she retained the secret knowledge that, in spite of appearances to the contrary, she had not dealt with Josephine efficiently upstairs, as her husband had expected her to. All that business about being a baby, and Roger some kind of child abductor! Nevertheless, Mrs Daley wondered whether, unsupervised, she might be on her way to a cure. Josephine needed a firm hand – she always had. It seemed to her there was a chance that, if Josephine suffered sufficient pain, she might transmogrify: this had been a theory she had held when Josephine was a child, and it involved a certain washing of one's hands, a consignment of things to a place of no hope. Let Josephine cry her tears – at some point they would run out.

The pastry was perfect. She stamped out one little round after another. They reminded her of babies, blank, circular, anonymous. She patted each one into its cup.

Considering everything, it didn't surprise Mrs Daley that she had forgotten to buy tights. Her outfit depended on a pair of black nylons, and in her drawer there were only blue. It seemed to her that she had been overtaxed. There were so many important things, but she, surely, was the most important – and it was herself she had in the end forgotten. She was completely unprepared for the contingency of having to wear something else; she had left herself time only for a series of military manoeuvres, diligently planned and practised, by which she had intended to assemble her appearance. She wasted half of this time turning out the drawer, unprepared to accept that what she needed wasn't there, and the rest in panicked consultation with her memory, which she hoped would yield up something of the necessary relevance, namely the recollection of a past incident, a social occasion on which she had worn an outfit involving blue. This incident, with its campaign notes, could not be retrieved. In a sweating flurry, filled with bitterness, the taste of bile on her tongue, she improvised. The result was strange; her inspiration had deserted her. It seemed all right in the bedroom, but then out in the hall, passing the mirror, she saw that she was emanating curious signals. Something was malfunctioning – was it her skirt? She moved on quickly, unhappily.

And now, in the kitchen, at a quarter past six, with people arriving at any minute, Roger and Josephine were boiling the kettle and getting out bottles and tins of powdered milk for the baby! And what a sight they were, Roger in his jeans and Josephine dragging about in the same unsavoury skirt she'd been wearing all week – Mrs Daley's ambition groaned beneath the weight of it all, in spite of the unexpected triumph of Roger's presence at her party, accompanied by a Josephine who was, if not exactly resplendent, at least dry-eyed. After the things Josephine had said, Mrs Daley had wondered whether they would be seeing Roger again, and whether it might not be better if they didn't. She had been surprised to discover that privately she found this prospect not unwelcome, the prospect of a woman alone. She would never have chosen such a life for herself, but she was mildly excited by the thought of Josephine living it.

It had turned out not to be like that, though. It had turned out that Roger knew all about Josephine and her strange feelings. He had driven down that morning to retrieve her and the baby, and had promptly told the Daleys that he hadn't thought it was a good idea for Josephine to come to Ravenley in the first place. According to him, Josephine had said she needed some head space, whatever that meant, and he hadn't wanted to block her. It struck Mrs Daley as being in some way distasteful, the way they spoke about each other. She and her husband had lived together for thirty-five years without speaking so; they had built their marriage on the rock of mutual privacy. She could have told them, if they'd asked her, why their lives were always collapsing around their ears, but they didn't ask. Nevertheless, having given up hope of normality where Josephine was concerned, she was determined at least to commemorate it on this occasion. She didn't care what Josephine did with her life after nine o'clock that evening, but until then Mrs Daley regarded it as her show. Besides, she was proud of Roger, in spite of the jeans. His exhibition had been reviewed in all the newspapers. An emerging talent, they had said, or something like that; things which, though superficially pleasing, irritated Mrs Daley now with the suggestion that nothing had been entirely accomplished and efforts remained to be made.

'Would you mind,' she said, 'not starting all that now? I've just got the kitchen tidy and people will be coming at any minute.'

'Well, how are we supposed to feed her?' said Josephine.

'I don't know,' snapped Mrs Daley. 'You'll have to find some other way.'

Reeling about the room on her way to the door she caught sight of Josephine slowly shaking her head from side to side, her mouth agape. She regained the empty, peach-toned sepulchre of the hall. Her husband was nowhere to be seen. Where had he got to? All this time she had been going about her preparations in the faith that he, her twin, was somewhere occupied in a parallel existence, that they were separate but harmonious in their movements, like workers in neighbouring fields; but now a silence seemed to be radiating from the core of the house, a central inactivity. Mrs Daley stood in the hall, listening, like the captain of a ship detecting trouble in the engine room. She felt the presence of a catastrophe, somewhere nearby. She searched the sitting room, the dining room – he had laid out the glasses there, at least – and with a sigh that came out as a strange, hoarse groan she began to make her way back upstairs, expecting to find him there but with no idea of why. Perhaps he had been taken ill; if so, how would she manage, alone? Pausing at an upstairs window to close the curtains, she saw a light in the garden. It spilled across the snow through the darkness, a whitish oblong stain. A fist of fury closed around Mrs Daley's heart. She turned around and thundered back down the stairs, passing Josephine and Roger coming up with the baby. They had their arms full of things, like burglars. Mrs Daley saw, dimly, that Roger was carrying the kettle. Its black lead and plug bumped up the carpeted stairs behind them. They said something to her but she did not hear it; she rushed down and through the hall and out the back door into the garden, where her patent-leather court shoes bit into the frozen crust of snow with a wet crunch and sank, and the black, cold night poured in a torrent through her clothes. Halfway across the lawn she thought that she should go back – the snow had soaked her tights up to the ankle – but the impossibility of her husband's presence in his shed seemed to spawn other impossibilities. Her labouring legs strained at the seams of her skirt. Panting, she bent forward to make herself go faster. When she got there she flung open the door without knocking, or looking through the window, and was therefore strangely surprised to see her husband sitting calmly in his chair staring straight ahead. He was wearing the clothes he had been wearing all day. A number of enquiries pumped from her mouth like blood from a wound, silently. Why was he not dressed? Why was he sitting out here, when he was urgently required elsewhere? What had happened? What had she done, this time, to displease him?

'What are you doing?' she cried.

'I'm thinking,' said her husband.

He presented himself to her stolidly. Out here, unbeknown to her, things had come to a head. The poison of a thousand moments had been drawn up into this far-flung, obstinate imperfection.

'About what?' she said.

'About my life.'

It was very cold in the shed. Mrs Daley chaffed at the thin arms of her blouse. The site of his disaffection was inhospitable. The lamp gave out a stark white light. There was nowhere for her to sit. These were the extreme conditions, she understood, of her husband's heart; but it all lay off to one side of her, a detached and chaotic region, a strife-torn country where at this precise moment she had neither the time nor the inclination to bring about peace. Her tights were wet; her shoes were ruined; her hair stood in frozen tufts on her head: she had suffered enough.

'I was thinking,' continued Mr Daley, 'that I might go.'

'Go where?'

'Somewhere else,' said Mr Daley.

'Where would you go?' said Mrs Daley scornfully. 'Who would have you?'

'I was thinking that I might go to Roger and Josephine.'

'Why on earth would you want to do that?'

'I think,' he reflected, as though he had all the time in

the world to do so, 'that their relationship is close to ideal.'

'That's not my impression of the situation!' Mrs Daley retorted.

Her husband considered this. His face was grey with the effort of emotion. Why did he cause himself this pain? He seemed so unfortunate. He was like an injured animal, lying in the grass listening to the tramp of the hunter's boots coming towards him.

'You've taken my soul away,' he said.

'I haven't touched your soul!' she cried.

'I wish I had thought about it,' he said dolefully. 'About my soul. And yours.'

Mrs Daley opened her mouth to say that she didn't have a soul, but a feeling stopped her. It was not a pleasant feeling. It reminded her of certain indignities that fell to the lot of women, instances of invasion – her husband's body, the doctor's gloved hand, three babies who had passed through her like boulders, like bulldozers.

'It all might have been different, you see. Instead it's driven us both mad.'

'What has?' exclaimed Mrs Daley.

'Marriage.'

'Oh, marriage!' she said. 'You never seemed all that interested in marriage!'

'I didn't think you had to be. I didn't know. I thought we were just doing what everybody else did.'

'We were!'

'Well, they were wrong too. We were all wrong.'

Mrs Daley looked at her watch. It was half past six. She felt the fact of the party arrive: it settled on her, momentously, like a bird with great wings.

'I am going in,' she declared. 'People will be arriving.'

Her voice was clear: behind it were the massed forces of fact and reason, of concrete things. She stood at the head of this army as its general; she showed her husband her power and waited to see what he would do. Presently, as she knew he would, her husband slowly rose, but before he had entirely left his chair Mrs Daley had turned and run back outside towards the house.

She did not think about that conversation with her husband again. It had not possessed sufficient clarity to make its way to the vault of memory. She couldn't make head nor tail of it; she had tossed it aside. And so many other things had happened that evening: life had risen like a great wave and dashed the little structures of nearby days. The party had been a great success. The Porters had come, and had glittered at the centre of it all. She'd since heard that Victor Porter was terribly ill, poor man, which explained the look of him. She often reflected that her party must have been one of their last public appearances. Her heart went out to Serena, it really did. To lose your husband, when you were still young and beautiful and the whole of life lay before you!

The one sour note had been the accident, which Mrs Daley had worried people might somehow think was her fault. Everyone agreed that they would never forget the sight of Colin Healey staggering into the drawing room with blood on his face and announcing that he'd killed his wife. Vanessa wasn't dead at all, but still, it was very dramatic. The car had gone off the road in the ice when they were on their way home and they'd hit a tree. She had heard rumours, she wouldn't say from whom, that all was not as it should have been in that marriage. Indeed, earlier in the evening they had argued conspicuously in Mrs Daley's hall and had left in a hurry: for a moment it all looked rather suspicious. Vanessa was in hospital now with a broken leg and an injured back. Mrs Daley had heard that her face was dreadfully scarred and that she would never recover the sight in one eye. As she said to Josephine on the telephone, it should make you think twice before complaining about your lot.

Matters of Life and Death

It was in the mornings that Vanessa most often suspected the existence of a problem. In the rumpled dawn camouflage of her bed she would open her eyes and think of the coming day and sometimes, just as when sometimes she turned the key in the ignition of her old Honda, nothing would happen. She lay there, paralysed by the image of what she had both to construct and then to dismantle before being returned to this same bed, like a book being returned to its shelf, intact and yet somehow depleted of her information.

Such thoughts usually caused her to give the key another turn, for though they seemed true in fact they were not: the complexity, the beloved texture of her life would resurge in their wake, unblocked, catalysed, assertive. It was true that a day spent with children had certain properties whose mastery amounted to an obscure science: but this science, being her work, her area of competence, performed the function of covering her nakedness. Vanessa had not particularly liked being in the world naked. Being a single woman had seemed to her overrated. During those years she had often had the sensation of being, involuntarily, in mid-air; of having been forced to jump not yet knowing whether anything would present itself for her to land on. She had not found this an exhilarating sensation. Also, she had within her a feeling of art, a desire for self-expression. When would she be availed of a canvas, a lump of clay, upon which to exercise these urges? She had worried that life would pass her by, and she was not alone: many of her female friends had said the same thing. In a very few cases these fears had been realised, which was sad. No one, Vanessa included, had ever believed that Vanessa would be alone, but she had worried enough to make her unsentimental. She knew herself well and she knew her enemy.

This enemy was not her husband; it was the capacity in herself, of which she was aware, for finding her husband unsatisfactory. Vanessa had no intention of letting this capacity have its head, nor any fear that it might one day just bolt without her permission and carry her away with it. What she stood on her guard against was a degree of private pain that this dissatisfaction, and its public suppression, could cause. She allowed her thoughts about Colin their independence, within a context of confinement: she monitored them at the root, if not at the source. Their source – Colin – was beyond her jurisidiction. Instead she had erected around them a blockade of certainty, this certainty being that she would never, could never, for reasons that to Vanessa were matters of life and death, leave Colin, and that her thoughts about him, in the absence of any practical means of annihilating them, would have instead to be indefinitely imprisoned. Allowing these thoughts to live constituted a whole region of Vanessa's moral existence. A discourse that could almost be described as spiritual had grown between herself and them. They furnished her inner world with beautiful forms, silent sculptures of lamentation and suffering. She walked among them, and by no word or gesture let Colin or anyone else know that they were there.

On this particular Thursday morning in October, for example, the baby, Danny, had begun to cry from his cot in the room next door, and because she felt unable to move she might have wished that Colin, who lay beside her with his head under the pillow, could have gone and got Danny himself. This was not only unlikely; it was unprecedented. Colin slept heavily in the mornings until past eight o'clock, before rising, silent and moody, to drink a cup of black coffee in the kitchen as he passed through it on his way to the door. Vanessa could suppress her wish, could cast it, as she might have cast a shred of paper from the deck of an ocean liner, into the churning wake below, with a generous, almost an exultant gesture. Nobody is perfect, she thought; we all have our good points and bad points; there are probably things about me—

'Can't you stop that child crying?' said Colin roughly, from beneath his pillow.

'I'm going,' said Vanessa, folding back the bedclothes.

Ten or so paces separated her bedside from Danny's room; on mornings such as this one, when Colin was difficult to explain away, these paces could have traversed a frozen plain on whose far side stood a warm shelter. This shelter was Vanessa's love for her children: she felt its firm qualities in direct proportion to the extremity of outside conditions. Now, for example, she moved towards it full of needs that required immediate relief. Danny was standing up in his cot with a face beautifully recast by sleep. They clasped one another, inaudibly to Colin in the next door room, and after some minutes progressed to the third bedroom, where Justin was sitting up in his little bed. Discovering her children thus, Vanessa experienced the pleasure of the treasure hunt: there they were in their beds, like jewels in their caskets, all hers, their finder's. It was difficult to believe, seeing them, as yet unsullied by the business of living, that they had ever tried her patience. These were the good moments, the gold: sometimes, she and the other mothers she knew confessed these moments to one another, shyly, as they might have confessed their feelings about men, which had once passed through the prism of incident in much the same way, that is, briefly but to profound effect. It didn't take much to lift Vanessa's love to the status of a preoccupying passion: a single glance from Justin or Danny, at bedtime, when nothing more could happen to dim the impression, could give her something to think about later, when she was lying next to Colin in the dark and groping in her thoughts for the centre of her being, alarmed by the possibility that it might not be there. She would remember the glance, or phrase, or gesture of affection, and there in the dark she would smile.

The three of them were sitting at the kitchen table when Colin passed through, dressed in his winter uniform of jeans and a black polo-neck sweater – in summer it was jeans and a white shirt – on his way to the office. Colin ran a company that made documentary films for television. He rented a unit in a building in town, where in times of famine his sole employee was an answering machine. When Colin was in a project, as he expressed it, he immediately created a new world of work, much as Vanessa created a day, out of thin air. He hired people, he rented space and equipment, he manufactured bustle and drama and strain, all of which would shrink, upon conclusion of a film, back to the small fixed point of his unit. Vanessa knew when they were in a project, as she would have known when she was in a storm, without needing to go out in it. The reality of days in the office she found harder to apprehend. She suspected these were interstices, during which Colin occupied himself in the way she had seen night-fishermen do on beaches, by planting himself in one spot, casting his line out to sea, and waiting.

'I'm going up to London today,' he said. He looked around and then back at her, raising his hands palm-up. 'Coffee?'

'Sorry. I'll get it.'

'I've got meetings, so you won't be able to get hold of me.'

'Anything interesting?' Vanessa enquired, but then Danny dropped his cereal bowl on the floor, spattering its contents over Vanessa's bare legs, and while she was clearing it up she missed his answer.

Colin ruffled the boys' hair and bent over to kiss her. She looked up in time to see his large face bearing down on her, with round eyes and pursed lips, and a tremor of aversion went unexpectedly through her.

'Are you going to spend the day in your dressing gown?' said Colin, in a manner that was neither malevolent nor comic but somewhere in between. His face remained close to hers.

'Of course not,' she said. 'Don't be ridiculous.'

'I just wondered,' said Colin.

'Well, don't wonder,' she said, while forcefully reminding herself that by ceasing to reply she would bring this undesirable exchange to an end.

'I don't think it's unreasonable of me,' pronounced Colin presently, with an excited look in his eyes, for he rarely climbed the ladder of debate this far with Vanessa, 'to expect my wife to make an effort when she sees me off to work in the morning.'

'What difference does it make?' replied Vanessa.

She said it without thinking, but it was clear as soon as the words were out of her mouth that they had come unauthorised from the place of detention. Her feeling of aversion at the sight of Colin's face, close up, returned to her: it struck her that she might be being punished for this feeling, if not by Colin then by some other power. Colin digested Vanessa's remark with the expression of a dog realising that what he had thought was a stick was in fact a bone.

'You tell me,' he replied, with a confused, victorious air.

He left the house, slamming the door behind him. Vanessa remained in her place at the kitchen table. In front of her lay the detritus of breakfast, which she had produced and which now she had to make vanish. The problem with turmoil of any sort was that such tasks became unbearable. It was for this reason that turmoil was something she generally avoided. She knew, as a matter of instinct, the position from which it was possible for her to take pleasure from her life: the good things, the right things, were like the sun, and in order to feel their warmth one had to avoid obstruction; one had to situate oneself far from the shade. It was perverse wilfully to cast oneself into that darkness, that cold. Sitting there at the table, she took a moment to convert herself back to her belief in Colin. It was not unreasonable that Colin should expect her to make an effort with her appearance. He was artistic: he cared about the look of things; disorder and neglect pained and troubled him. This was the way he was, and there was no point in wishing that he were some other way. Vanessa rose and began to clear the table. Her heart had ceased to pound. The sun's rays, weak but getting warmer, were on her once more. She lifted

Danny from his highchair, where he had used her moments of distraction to spread butter over his face and hair unimpeded, and held him close. He laughed and patted her face with his greasy palms. Treacherously, she revelled in the mess on her cheeks. With Colin out of the house she generally felt free to prosecute such treachery, but this morning, after their argument, she felt guilty. She and Colin were due a period of realignment, an interlude in which she checked her drift towards the children. Vanessa had found it difficult to keep these allegiances fixed. The part of her that yearned to be on the children's side, to be one of them, was directly fuelled by her daily exposure to Colin and to what he was – a man and hence different from her – while her romantic attachment to Colin these days drew nearly all its strength from her desire to set apart from herself the children and the work of looking after them. She didn't feel this desire very often. It was their innocence, she supposed. Being close to Colin necessarily involved striking a position of ignorance of, or indifference to, this innocence. It involved a feat of concealment, an effort. Forgetting Colin required no such effort, although it had certain practical consequences, such as those to which this morning he had taken exception.

It seemed to Vanessa that she should do something to please Colin on his return from work, and this ambition immediately rose like a great spire from the humble structure of the day. Colin did not acknowledge mere sufficiency: what he liked was something extra, an aspect of miracle. He liked to be surprised, or thought he did. Vanessa sometimes suspected that Colin didn't entirely know who he was: surprises, while paying him the tribute of suggesting that someone else at least knew who he was, could also cause him anxiety. For example, Vanessa had once bought him a black Labrador puppy, as a surprise, and he had been moved to tears by her gesture, for he had often said – and as far as he knew it was true – that he had wanted a dog since boyhood but had never been allowed to have one. Colin's relations with this puppy, however, were volatile. It irritated him and made messes everywhere; its hair made him sneeze. Eventually his demeanour became that of a person who disliked dogs altogether, and the fact that the dog remained in the house was presented to other people as evidence of Vanessa's intransigence, perhaps even her cruelty. One day Vanessa took the dog away and left it grimly at the pound.

She ascended the stairs with Danny in her arms and Justin scrambling behind her. The curtains in her bedroom were still closed and the bed was unmade. Colin's crumpled pyjamas lay across it, like the discarded skin of a snake. The air was heavy with the scent of bodies. Colin had escaped, leaving her like a big spider in its web. She dressed and tidied up as quickly as she could, trying not to breathe; and, hurling her dressing gown, still warm, into the laundry basket, she hoped that she had put her disagreement with Colin, and its murky justice, behind her. Seized by sanitary fury, she moved on to the bathroom, excising hairs and fingerprints, folding towels, opening windows. She toured the boys' rooms, making beds, folding, putting away. The boys followed in her wake, eddying around her feet, quivering behind her like ripples as she stalked away. Vanessa was used to working in this element, which lapped continually around her calves. Occasionally the boys grabbed at her legs and tried to make her stand still. Her motion worked on them in phases, at first soothing, then increasingly unsustainable, until they seemed filled with a strange electricity and grew frantic, needing to touch her as if to earth themselves. Vanessa had their music inside her. She spoke and responded automatically, like someone who bypasses thought in order to reach their gift. They progressed in their whirling formation back down the stairs and span around the sitting room, the boys displacing and Vanessa putting back. Her goal was the front door and after that the car, where she would put the boys in their seats and drive them to the supermarket in order to purchase the ingredients of the special dinner with which she had decided to present Colin when he returned from work. In the kitchen she observed his coffee cup, which stood with its black dregs on the sideboard, where he had left it. Seeing it, Vanessa was struck again by aversion; a deep and poisonous shaft of it shot through her. By washing the cup up she could return it to its neutral condition, but it seemed to her to be broadcasting contamination, to be untouchable.

'Come on,' she said to Justin, holding his coat in front of him.

'Where are we going?' he said.

'To the shops,' she replied, filled with tenderness and pity for him, for never knowing where they were going, for living each minute with no idea of what was going to happen in the next. It was in these moments that she couldn't understand how mothers left their children with other people, how they could bear to confound this simple blindness, this expectation that things would remain the same.

'I don't want to go,' said Justin, hitting the coat so that it flapped in her hands.

A fork in the road appeared before Vanessa's eyes. The hitting stabbed at her; violent feelings seeped hotly from the wound. She saw herself throwing the coat across the room, and as clearly saw the other, peaceful route of which she was simultaneously availed.

'It'll be fun,' she said.

'OK,' said Justin: it was that easy, Vanessa thought. 'But I don't want to wear my coat.'

'OK,' said Vanessa. It was, again, so simple: it was a mere matter of giving the appearance of concession, while retaining the intention not to concede anything. She didn't believe that she was deceiving her children by this practice. She was simply helping them to manage their emotions. By the time they arrived at the supermarket, Justin would have forgotten that he didn't want to wear his coat, and would wear it happily. She picked up Danny and led Justin out of the front door.

Outside it was bright and windy: the trees and the little lane and the church stood in sharp light, wetly, like things that had just been born. Big dark-grey clouds sagged at the horizon. Shafts of glare were suspended from the sky at angles to the hillside. Strands of Vanessa's hair whipped against her face as she bent to put the boys into the back seat. Standing up again, she saw Victor Porter in the lane, walking in her direction.

'It's quite a business,' he said pleasantly, 'isn't it? When I go somewhere on my own now I have to keep stopping because I think I've left something behind.'

She realised that he was speaking about the children.

'Although it's rather appealing,' he added, peering in through the window of the car, 'having them trussed up.'

'They'll avenge themselves at the supermarket,' said Vanessa, although this was not the way in which she usually spoke.

Victor stared at something above and beyond her. Vanessa was struck by his paleness: his skin looked rough and bloodless, almost sickly.

'The outside world,' he said. 'I'd almost forgotten it was there.'

'Perhaps it isn't, any more,' said Vanessa.

'Let me know,' Victor laughed, raising his hand and walking slowly away.

Vanessa got in the car and put her hands to her cheeks, which were burning. She hardly knew Victor – in fact, she couldn't now think of another occasion on which she had spoken to him alone. He and his wife had been weekenders in the village for three or four years, except that they hadn't seemed to come much at weekends either. The square pink house behind the church stood empty for month after month, rain falling disconsolately on its roof, or the sun beating down on the deserted garden; and then suddenly, out of the blue, the overgrown driveway would be packed with smart cars and the sounds of unfamiliar voices would ring around the village. Someone had told her a few weeks ago that the Porters were moving down permanently, but she had forgotten it, or hadn't believed it. It seemed un- likely, at least as far as his wife was concerned. Vanessa had only ever met her on the steep, narrow roads outside the village, when they were both in their cars, and Serena Porter, driving too fast, would flash past her, unseeing, her mouth set in a line. Through the car windows she looked fragile and beautiful, like something kept behind glass. Apparently she wrote for a newspaper, but Vanessa didn't read newspapers.

She drove to the supermarket, where she felt marginally but strangely outside her own body, rather weightless and dashing, so that it surprised her to remember that she was unable to go, as she suddenly had the impulse to, to a café in the centre of town and drink coffee on her own. The children and the dinner she had to cook rested lightly but precariously on her: she felt forgetful of them, unconnected, as though she might simply walk off. She drove back to the village with a spring of frustration wound in her chest, and when she saw Colin's coffee cup still on the sideboard emotion surged to her head, mercurial, pungent, making her eyes water.

At twelve o'clock she gave the boys their lunch, mashing up food for the baby slowly with a fork. Danny wailed like a siren and pounded his fists in his bowl. Justin giggled manically, watching her wipe up the mess, and began to throw everything that was on the table on to the floor. No forked path appeared to Vanessa now, merely a straight, pounding motorway that offered no opportunity for getting off. She struggled in the kitchen as if in a snare, searching for some mechanism that might free her. She succeeded in detaching Danny and Justin from the table and isolating them in a corner of the kitchen by the sink. She wiped the food from their hands and faces and then, keeping them behind her, advanced on her hands and knees towards the table with her cloth. Danny grabbed the back of her sweater and pulled himself to a standing position, while Justin encircled her neck with his arms and lifted his feet from the floor. Vanessa extended her arm and removed the clods of food from the floor beneath the table without moving. She rarely permitted things to progress to this point: very soon she would have to reassert her control of the situation. She told Justin to stay where he was and took Danny upstairs in order to put him in his cot. Danny roared as soon as he understood his fate, which was to sleep, but Vanessa insisted, she prevailed, and Danny began to subside; but then Justin, whom she had momentarily forgotten, was heard ascending the stairs, emitting loud sounds of distress. She dashed to the door in the hope of waylaying him, but he burst in before she got there, his face a wreck of tears, at which sight Danny bayed and wept in solidarity and Vanessa felt, finally, defeated.

Downstairs, later, with Danny asleep and Justin playing, Vanessa considered the silence of the telephone, which Colin might have used to make things right between them, instead of leaving her all day with no recourse, no outlet, no way of moving on from the discord in which he had marooned her that morning, while he drifted untethered about the capital. It was unlikely that Colin had taken this view of her predicament: if anything, he regarded the odds as being decisively stacked against him in the politics of their household. More or less, Vanessa agreed with him: it was understood between them that Vanessa's position in the world represented a kind of ultimate leisure. It was something that he, Colin, had purchased for her. Vanessa invested her days with sufficient sincerity that it didn't much matter how she had come by them, but she often found herself occupied with the question of what she owed Colin in return, and what he continued to owe her notwithstanding. His not phoning, like her wearing the dressing gown, seemed to indicate that he didn't care about her. Vanessa considered this interesting possibility while assisting Justin in the construction of a small tower on the kitchen floor. Once, a few years before, when she had been pregnant with Justin, she had left Colin for a total of three hours. It was shortly after they had moved to the village, and perhaps it was being in a new house that had caused a glaring light to fall on everything they had introduced into it; but Vanessa, inferring strong nuances of inescapability from her swelling stomach, had in this light perceived that she did not want to spend the rest of her life with Colin. While he was at work she had got into the car and driven almost all the way to London, where one or two of her friends lived; and then she had turned around and driven weeping all the way back. She had not understood then how men pass through you, so that you and first one child and then another are strung along them like beads on a thread. The presence of Colin inside her, unexpurgated, had seemed to her monstrous, but then the baby had come and that line, that thread, so distressing while in the act of being drawn through her, now caused her so little sensation that she could hardly be said to feel it at all. She had never, of course, told Colin about that drive. Perhaps she should have, she didn't know: honesty had a certain appeal; it changed things, but not necessarily for the better.

She began to cook but a lack of conviction made her dither, so that when Danny woke and Justin grew bored she found that she had created chaos but made little progress towards resolving it. Similarly, in her deliberations about Colin she had established that something was wrong but not what it was. She considered that he might, in London, or in any of the places he went unobserved by her, form emotional ties to other people, and was surprised immediately to discover that she couldn't have cared less if he did, that she would positively welcome a development of this sort, relieving her as it would of the burden of Colin's feelings, of the business of pleasing him in ways that didn't please herself, of the way he operated as the neglected child of her conscience when she had real children, actual children, to take care of.

She took these children for a walk outside, to cool herself off. Justin's cries as he straggled behind her on the lane seemed to have steel in them, so sharply did they cut her ears. Danny sat like a rock in his pushchair. They reached the gate that led to the field behind the church, and went in. This field bordered the garden of the Porters' house, and Vanessa reflected that it would not have displeased her at this moment to encounter Victor again. A nebulous feeling of daring possessed her: there appeared to be some pause, some interval in her relations with the children, during which she felt she might, briefly, absent herself with the prospect of getting further than she usually did. It seemed to her that Victor had played her a tune that she couldn't quite remember and wanted to hear again. She had not had this experience often in her life, although she had it with her children. It was a shame, she thought now, that she had noticed it about Victor: her noticing was the warrant which imminently would send this feeling to the place of detention. While it wandered so pleasantly free, it would have warmed her to meet him, but she did not; she rallied, there in the field, and played football with Justin while Danny crawled around and put things in his mouth. The wind had dropped; the clouds were netted back at the horizon. Black rooks made ragged holes in the pale autumn sky. When it was time to go, Vanessa picked Danny up and held out her hand to Justin. At that moment, she heard a woman's voice nearby say, 'Snap.' She looked up and saw Serena Porter standing in her garden on the other side of the fence. She had a baby on her hip and a little girl stood beside her. She was looking straight at Vanessa.

'I said, Snap. A matching set. Two each.'

She was tall and thin, with red hair that fell over her shoulders, and a pale face with a slightly crooked mouth. When she smiled, she showed eye teeth like tiny fangs.

'Mine are boys,' said Vanessa.

It sounded rude, and Vanessa saw something pass quickly over Serena's face, an adjustment, like the clicking figures on the boards of financial markets.

'Would they like to come and play?' she said.

'We have to get home,' said Vanessa.

'Oh, I didn't mean now. But one afternoon? What's your name?' she said, to Justin.

'This is Justin, and Danny,' said Vanessa.

'Well, Justin and Danny, this is Margret and Frances and they'd like you to come and have tea with them tomorrow. Is tomorrow all right?'

'I think that would be all right,' said Vanessa. 'What time?' she persisted, although she sensed that Serena Porter's attention had departed.

'I don't know,' said Serena. 'Teatime. Whenever you're ready.'

She turned and wandered back into her garden like an exotic creature returning to its habitat. Vanessa walked slowly home, lightly plagued by feelings of excitement and dread. She washed up Colin's coffee cup and made dinner. Later, she fed the children and put them to bed. By the time Colin came back she was no longer fully able to grasp the purpose of the celebration she was imposing on him. The morning's dispute seemed dull and representational; the life had passed out of it. Colin, standing in the kitchen, seemed like all the Colins she had ever known and no particular one of them. He was big, anomalous, vaguely contoured, the landscape of her life. He'd had a bad day; the meetings had not gone well. The channel didn't want his film and for now there was nowhere else to take it. A period of financial uncertainty lay ahead of them. He told her this while eating the food she had cooked without remark. She let him eat, having decided not to mention that there was anything to remark on.

'Which house is yours?' said Serena Porter, standing at her kitchen window with her arms folded, like a passenger on a cruise ship wishing to have the landmarks pointed out to her by a member of the crew.

'The white cottage,' said Vanessa. 'The one on the right just before that barn.'

'Sweet,' said Serena, turning away.

A gust of wind blew a splat of rain against the window. The Porters' house was not what Vanessa had been expecting. The garden was wild, and coming in Vanessa had caught sight of big, unruly rooms. As for the kitchen, it looked like somewhere where a violent scene had just occurred. Toys lay on their sides all over the floor. Dirty dishes, nappies and newspapers covered every surface. The ruins of lunch remained on the table. Justin and Danny crawled around in it, like scavengers picking over a wreck. The girls, Margret and Frances, were sitting back to back beneath the table. Frances was silently chewing an envelope. Margret was methodically dropping marbles into a cup with a series of clicks, and thrusting her small fist in to take them out again.

'My husband's in London,' stated Serena, as though this explained everything.

Frances, the baby, started to cry and Serena knelt down to get her out from under the table. As she withdrew her she banged the baby's head against the tabletop. Frances bawled, putting her hand to her head.

'Oh, I'm sorry!' cried Serena, hugging the writhing body. 'I'm sorry!'

'What did you do?' said Margret, twisting round and knocking over the cup of marbles with her foot so that they scattered with a sibilant sound across the floor. 'Mummy, what did you do?'

The telephone started to ring in the hall. Serena got up with Frances still in her arms and went to answer it. As she reached the door her foot slid on one of the marbles and she staggered to one side, her red hair flying out, her thin, dark-clad body forking out like a twig with the fat pink blossom of the baby shaking on her hip.

'Let's pick these up, shall we?' said Vanessa when she was gone. She held out her hand to Margret for the cup. The child looked at her with large, suspicious eyes and surrendered it. Vanessa began to trawl the floor for the marbles.

'– completely unsentimental,' she heard Serena say from the hall. 'Completely.'

'Boys,' said Vanessa. 'Do you want to help me pick these up?'

'– mine is the only authentic consciousness,' said Serena. 'So I can see that we're doomed but nobody else can, and somehow I'm going to have to persuade them that we are, at which point we'll move back to London—'

Once she had established the children picking up the marbles Vanessa moved to the counters and began to stack up the dirty dishes. A shadow fell across the window and the rain came down in a rush. She looked out and saw the trees waving their arms wildly in the wind, then bending away as though to shield themselves from blows. Beyond them, through the veil of rain, she saw the white square of her house. Its windows stared straight ahead, like eyes.

'– an art form. Victor's brilliant at it . . . No, lives that are lived unconsciously, unpolitically – and I'm talking about the women rather than the men.' She paused and then laughed. 'He might as well have a tail.'

'Mummy,' said Justin. 'I want a drink.'

She put the dishes in the sink and turned on the taps. The water rose, hesitating at the rims of things and then pouring over in a flood. Justin placed his hand softly on the back of her leg. He did it as someone might lean against a wall, to rest. Steam rose from the water into Vanessa's face. Her son's hand remained on her leg. She felt stationary, monumental, like some object in nature buffeted by weather. Out in the hall she heard Serena hang up.

'Sorry,' she called. 'My editor. He always phones at exactly the worst time and then doesn't believe me when I say I've got to go. He thinks the children are figments of my imagination.'

'I want a drink,' said Justin.

'Oh, *leave* that,' said Serena, placing a hand on Vanessa's arm. 'Please. You're making me feel awful. I've trained myself not to see it. I realised a few years ago that it was the kitchen or me, a straight fight. And I won.'

'Don't worry,' said Vanessa. 'It'll just take a minute.'

'I want a drink,' said Justin.

'I want a drink too,' said Margret.

Vanessa took her hands out of the hot water and went to the fridge.

'Do yours have milk?' she said.

'Thanks, yes,' said Serena. 'Whatever there is. Thank you.'

Vanessa poured the milk and gave it to the children.

'How long have you lived in Ravenley?' said Serena. She folded her arms and scrutinised Vanessa as though she were a problem or puzzle that needed solving.

'Four years.'

'We've been coming here for almost that,' said Serena. 'But I don't think I've ever seen you. We don't really know anybody here. We just sort of packed up and left London in a rush. Victor's taken some time off work,' she added, 'and I can work anywhere.'

'What is it,' said Vanessa, 'that you do?'

'I write a newspaper column.'

'What about?'

'Well,' said Serena with a laugh. 'It's about – life.'

'I don't really read newspapers,' said Vanessa. 'I never have the time.'

She realised that they were both shouting. It was the children, the noise they made – trying to talk was like swimming in a rough sea; you kept feeling it rising beneath you then hollowing out.

'It's a sort of diary,' Serena was saying. 'I'm trying to write about feminism in the context of the family. About how inequality runs through the veins of how we live together and love and reproduce. How it's experienced, if you like.'

'And what does your husband think about it?' smiled Vanessa. 'Does he mind?'

'No,' said Serena. She seemed surprised. 'Why should he? It's got nothing to do with him.'

'Because you must write at least a bit out of personal experience,' said Vanessa.

'He doesn't read everything I write. He agrees with most of it anyway.'

'How can he?' laughed Vanessa. 'He's a man.'

Serena smiled mysteriously and locked her long, pale fingers around her teacup.

'Do you think women actually want it?' said Vanessa. 'To be the same as men, or the other way around?'

'*I* do,' said Serena. 'Don't you?'

'Well,' said Vanessa, 'wouldn't it be a bit boring if everyone was the same?'

An expression of impatience flitted across Serena's face, which she had bent over her fingers as though in concentration or prayer.

'Go on,' she said.

'Well,' said Vanessa, 'there are things I really like about being at home with the children. Nobody tells me what to do; I'm pretty free to do as I like. I've got more independence here than I'd have in some office. And besides, what about the children? Where would they fit in? I didn't have them never to see them. They've got rights too.'

They both looked at the children, as though at the evidence for the prosecution.

'You might have independence,' said Serena. 'But you don't have freedom.'

'I don't want freedom,' said Vanessa. She folded her arms and looked at Serena with a small smile.

'Why not?' said Serena.

'I don't want to be alone,' said Vanessa.

'That's not what I mean,' said Serena. 'I mean equal.'

'But I am,' said Vanessa. 'I'm more than equal. I'm the lucky one.'

The telephone rang again in the hall and Serena went to answer it.

'Hi!' Vanessa heard her say in a breathy voice.

She stared at the children. Her head hurt and her mouth was dry. She felt disorientated; for a moment she couldn't think what they were all doing here.

'– convening the Ravenley sub-committee on the rights of housewives,' said Serena in the hall.

'Where's Mummy?' said Margret, looking around with a dazed expression.

Vanessa felt a surge of impatience. For a moment she could not reply. That was the difference between other people's children and her own, the numberless acts of love that occurred beyond the margins of her will.

'She'll be back in a minute,' she said.

'Oh,' said Margret. 'Who are you?'

'That was Victor,' Serena said peevishly when she came back. 'He's missed his train. I was supposed to get my column in this evening. Isn't it funny,' she added, 'how a man's time is always his own. In London we had a nanny. At least I knew she was doing it for the money. Whereas Victor *wants* to look after the children. There's a big,' she sighed, 'difference.'

'You're lucky that he wants to,' said Vanessa. 'Plenty of men don't.'

'They should *have* to,' said Serena sharply. 'There's no reason why a husband can't look after children while a wife works.'

'Colin wouldn't last a day,' Vanessa replied. 'That's not a criticism – it just isn't in his nature. And even if it was, isn't that just the same problem the other way around?'

'Are you sure that your natures are so different?'

'I don't think,' said Vanessa slowly, 'that I'd be able to respect him.'

Danny started to cry and Vanessa picked him up. The

feel of her baby, scented, hot, yielding, needy, drifted over her in an analgesic wave. The two older children began to shout, tugging a toy back and forth between them. Vanessa felt at the mercy of a process that was both necessary and scientific, as though, like someone on an operating table, she was the point at which numbing and cutting forces converged.

'Justin,' she said, 'let that go.'

'Respect,' said Serena. 'That's the heart of it really, isn't it? The dark heart.'

'We ought to be going,' said Vanessa.

Serena followed them to the door, where Vanessa began to put the boys back into their wet coats. Justin kicked her and cried when she tried to force his arms into the sleeves. She put Danny bucking into his pushchair.

'Please,' said Serena. 'Can't I help you?'

Vanessa wrenched open the front door. The rain was falling in grey sheets over the garden. She held Justin by the wrist and he corkscrewed, dangling.

'You've already got your hands full,' said Vanessa.

'That's true,' said Serena consideringly. 'It just never feels that way.'

Justin had started waking up at night. Vanessa, lying in bed, would hear through muddled dreams the thud of his little feet hitting the floor in the next-door room and then the staccato sounds of running, noises which hurt her tired body and caused her sleeping mind painfully to revolve, like a cold engine turning over on a frosty morning. Her door would slowly open, letting in electric light from the hall, and Justin would present himself on the threshold, an unwelcome spectre of day. Again and again she would stagger through the thick dark to replace him in his room. Vanessa liked to explain to people her belief that since she gave herself entirely to her children during their waking hours, her nights were her own, but this belief, though she retained it as passionately as ever, seemed to have become involuntarily harmless. How had she ever enforced it? She couldn't remember. She had no weapons, no army. It seemed that for three years Justin had not woken up at night, and now, for no reason at all, he woke: it appeared that things changed. Colin had moved into the spare room, whose door was not left ajar. Like Justin, he was free to do as he liked; she couldn't stop him. Colin needed to sleep and Justin didn't. That was the state of things. That was the situation.

'It doesn't make any difference to you,' Colin said. 'You don't have to work.'

'Actually,' Vanessa replied, 'it is quite hard work, looking after the children.'

'All right then,' said Colin. 'You go and earn the money and I'll sit at home all day drinking coffee. I know which I'd rather do.'

They talked a lot about Colin's work at the moment. It had a sort of abstract quality: it was a symbol, an idea, and the more immaterial it became the more they talked about it. Vanessa sensed that the day was drawing near on which she would be able finally to refute this idea. Fact would be reprised; it had to be. Colin had given up his unit in town to save money and had set up an office at home, in the small room off the kitchen where Vanessa paid bills and did household accounts and kept things in an old filing cabinet. This filing cabinet, along with every other sign of her presence, had been ejected into the kitchen. The room was now

Colin's domain, that and the spare bed, where he passed his nights in thoughts and dreams that Vanessa tried to imagine but couldn't, for though his territories had shrunk he seemed to her more unguessable, more foreign, than ever before. She apprehended him now as a purely physical being: in the old days, when he had left the house, he had diffused in her mind into the outside world so that he became part of its importance, one of its many unknown quantities, and when he re-formed himself on his return he shone, like a star, with borrowed light. Now, finding him situated in one part or another of the house, his solidity oppressed her. He was parked there like a car, in the sitting room, in the kitchen. At first Vanessa had tried to keep the children quiet or take them out, but now she took them out only when it pleased her. The children were ineradicably factual. Colin would occasionally open his office door and bark at them to be quiet, but, as Vanessa remarked, he couldn't expect them to keep their lives on hold. Vanessa made cups of coffee for Colin and knocked at his door to deliver them. She wanted him to know that she, at least, still believed in that idea, his work. He was generally to be found on the telephone, or reading the newspaper.

Lately, though, Colin had started going out during the day, usually just before lunch. He disliked having lunch with the three of them, and Vanessa disliked it too. It removed yet another counterpoint from the day; it was almost embarrassing, the whole family sitting around the table at every meal, suggesting as it did that no one had anything better to do. But Colin's protracted, unexplained absences had a dampening effect on Vanessa. As soon as he went, some private exhilaration went with him. Her tiredness rose to her skin, suffusing her with gloom. She began to wonder what she had been thinking of, treating their problems as a game. The reality of the situation would show her its dark, its cavernous depths. She had assumed that something would happen to Colin – event was part of his personality, or she thought it was. He came home and said, I've sold an idea, or, We're going into production, and she received an impression of sport, of some competitive but friendly engagement with destiny, with fate, in which there were wins and losses and moments of heart-stopping worry or joy, but which never reached any meaningful resolution. She brought neither the conception of success nor that of failure to her perception of Colin's career, merely the expectation of continuity. But Colin, as he frequently reminded her, did not work in a bank. Tired as she was, she could not entirely remember why he didn't. Because he had an art; because he was gifted. She felt now that she had not attended sufficiently when he had explained this side of his character. She wasn't sure how interested she was in art, in gifts. If Colin couldn't find a buyer for these gifts, he would have to find some other occupation. This became abruptly and entirely clear to her. She wondered if it had yet made itself clear to him.

'Have you considered,' she said to him, 'looking for something else, just until everything sorts itself out?'

The day had come; the worm of fact had turned. Vanessa had received a bill printed in red, which Colin had forbidden her to pay.

'No,' said Colin.

'Well,' she said, after sufficient silence, 'what are we going to do for money?'

'You tell me,' said Colin.

He said this unpleasantly. The kitchen, with its wooden

dressers, its china, its pots and pans and fittings, its hum-ming dishwasher, its incidental lighting – all clean, all in order – seemed to stem from Vanessa like a great feathered tail, opulent, ludicrous. Her whole life just then stood around her like a projection, a fantasy, the work of a deluded mind. Had Colin wanted this? She wasn't sure. She had a desire to conceal it all from him, to render it blameless.

'I can't tell you,' she said.

'Why not?'

'Because I don't know.'

'Why don't you know?'

'Because that isn't our arrangement,' she said finally.

'Our arrangement,' he said, 'might have to change.'

That was all he said. He ate his food in silence and Vanessa watched a flush of obscure emotion rise up his face to the white dome of his forehead. Presently he got up and left the table, and she heard the soft thud of his footsteps going upstairs. She cleared the table, except for his plate, which she hated. It sat where he had left it, smeared with food, the knife and fork at aggressive angles. Vanessa felt the vertiginous presence of a precipice, somewhere nearby. It seemed to be emanating a white light of danger. How had she got so close to the end, the edge? She cleared the plate and went upstairs to her bed, which was empty. Colin's absence, although it did not surprise her, filled her suddenly with compunction and fear. She should go to him; she should offer herself to him, in surrender. A desire to lash herself to him came over her, because this was after all a storm and Colin, Colin was pitching about but he was seaworthy, he was afloat, he was the only protection she had, and if she felt free it was only the freedom of some-thing untethered on deck that at any moment would be washed overboard and left behind to sink into the cold, merciless depths. The problem was that if she spent the night in the spare room, Justin wouldn't be able to find her if he woke. Perhaps she would ask Colin to return with her to their room. She sensed that she would discover by this course of action something she did not want to know, which was that Colin found her concern for the children a turn-off, and that it had eaten so far into his interest in her that one more reminder of it would extinguish it altogether. She sat on her bed in her clothes. She did not weep, or put her head in her hands – she didn't feel like it. She merely sat for a while, and then she got undressed and got into bed and lay in the dark with her eyes open. Justin, that night, did not come in, and Vanessa woke with a feeling of steel in her, a feeling of independence, of having acted irreversibly, although she had, of course, she reminded herself, done nothing.

In the morning she took the boys up to Hill House with Danny's old pram, which Barbara Daley had asked if she could borrow because her daughter was coming to stay with her new baby. It was an old-fashioned pram with big steel wheels and springs. Vanessa had never been quite sure about it. It was a bit over the top; it seemed to make a statement where Vanessa felt there was no need to speak. She wheeled them up the hill, both sitting in it. It was the first time Vanessa had offered her children an activity of this sort. They were reverent with excitement, nearly silent as they bounced along: they looked around at the countryside, decaying and autumnal, shrouded in mist, with solemn, important faces. Whenever they caught her eye Vanessa felt she had been noticed acting strangely. Normally she would have put the pram in the back of the car and driven them up there: she was not a 'fun' mother, like some of the mothers she knew. It always seemed to her the final distinction, between herself and her children, that she was not a child. She regarded playful mothers as being in this important sense confused. Her love was safely enclosed in her authority, and although she visited in herself other, less structured desires, her boys never knew that she did. She discerned in these desires the potential for chaos. By resisting them, day in and day out, she had attained a state of refinement, and of abasement, too, of humility before the task of motherhood. It was a part of this humility that she felt entitled to judge other mothers. When she saw them shout, or smother, or complain, or draw attention to themselves the full weight of her sacrifice bore down on her. And something else, some sore of injured vanity was rubbed by it, for it was the essence of this sacrifice that it was silent and yet she always knew, every day, that she had made it: if there was to be acknowledgement, why was she, who was strong, not acknowledged? Now, though, she was pushing her children up the hill in a pram meant for a newborn baby and her children, though concerned, appeared to be finding something magical in the experience. She felt very slightly betrayed by them. Did they want her to be someone else, someone different? A heedless, romantic person who did adventurous, pointless things? Vanessa wondered what else this person might do. She lifted them out at Mrs Daley's gate and walked with them the rest of the way up the neatly gravelled drive.

'How did you get here?' cried Mrs Daley, opening the front door and immediately, it seemed to Vanessa, finding the situation suspicious.

'We walked,' Vanessa replied.

'Up that hill! I've never heard of such a thing! Why on earth would you want to do that?' She addressed this question to Danny. 'Well, you're here now. The kettle's just boiled. I think I might even have something nice for you two young men. Shall we go and see?'

She walked off, leaving Vanessa and the children standing on the doorstep with the pram.

'Do you want me to bring this in?' said Vanessa.

'Well, let's see,' said Mrs Daley, coming back. She regarded the pram with distaste. 'It's a great big thing, isn't it? I haven't seen one of these for years! I think, if you don't mind, that I'll ask Derek to wheel it round to the garage. The mud from the lane has got all over the wheels. You see, I thought you'd be bringing it in the car.'

Vanessa followed her into the house, which smelled of polish, and whose air was so free of dust and human presence and the sharp smells of outside that breathing it Vanessa felt slightly weightless. She had an impression of profound, oppressive order as she glimpsed Mrs Daley's rooms on her way through the hall, of time hanging heavy. She didn't know why – she had been to Mrs Daley's house before – but these rooms just now reminded her of how long life was: they stood around her, empty, immaculate, pointless, like things that had wildly revolved and then gradually, over time, ground to a halt. Mrs Daley, the curator of this stasis, seemed as she addressed Vanessa to be holding in her hands a fanatically embroidered solitude, a mad tapestry of self-reference, like the trails a caged creature makes in its own sawdust. Her face was boldly made-up; her hair stood in sculpted waves. Her eyes were wide open but glazed and unblinking: with the slightest tap, Vanessa thought, she would shatter into pieces. And yet there was something indestructible, too, some stubbornness at her core. Was that to be Vanessa's own destiny? That once this work of giving and sustaining life had ended, once this spinning motion had ceased, she would solidify into an eternal redundancy? Hauling Danny on her hip towards the kitchen, she did not feel like she was spinning. All the same, she had a strange feeling, about the future, which reached away like a dark hinterland from the safe settlement of the present moment. In the kitchen, Mrs Daley opened a tin of biscuits and held it out to the boys.

'Do they have these?' she asked Vanessa. 'Only I know that these days mothers can get very jumpy about what their children eat. Sometimes it seems as though there are so many things they're *not* allowed to eat that you can't think what on earth to give them. I have to be very careful with my grandchildren – there are five of them, well, six now, I suppose, all with different allergies, and I have to try not to get them muddled up. Just between you and me,' she continued, lowering her voice, 'I don't always succeed, and not one of them has ever showed the slightest sign of being allergic to anything. Don't tell their mothers I said that. It's terribly embarrassing when they have to go – they all want to stay, because they say the food's so much better here than it is at home!'

'When is your daughter coming?' said Vanessa.

'Any minute!' exclaimed Mrs Daley dramatically. 'I've always thought,' she added, 'that a woman needs her mother when she becomes a mother herself. Shall we get a cloth for those?' She bore down on Danny, who was sitting on the floor with his fingers covered with chocolate.

'Sorry,' said Vanessa, 'I'll do it.'

'No, no! You stay where you are. I'm quite used to children, with three of my own and five grandchildren. You sit and have your coffee. These are wonderful days, aren't they, but you don't get much of a chance to put your feet up!'

She wiped Danny's fingers firmly and he started to cry.

'Oh dear,' she said. 'I think someone wants Mummy.'

'We ought to go,' said Vanessa, picking him up. He squirmed violently in her lap.

'Stay where you are!' cried Mrs Daley. 'You young mothers never let yourselves relax. Josephine, my daughter, is constantly exhausted, and she's only got one tiny baby. I don't like to tell her that it gets worse once they're walking around and into everything.'

'Justin,' said Vanessa. 'Leave that.'

'The problem is,' said Mrs Daley, regretfully, 'that she's up with this baby all night, or so she says. It's never as bad as you think it is, is it? But she's got it into her head that she has to feed her whenever she cries, and so of course she's up every hour, and meanwhile the baby is having lots of fun making everyone run around and doesn't see why she should go to sleep.'

'Justin,' said Vanessa, while Danny flailed his arms in her lap. His fist struck her cheek.

'There seems to be this *mania* these days,' said Mrs Daley, 'for self-feeding, or breastfeeding, or whatever they call it now.'

'Yes,' said Vanessa.

'We never bothered with all that,' said Mrs Daley, with a little laugh. 'They told us our husbands wouldn't like it. That was the great thing, in those days, keeping your husband happy. No one seems to worry about that any more, which I suppose is why the divorce rate is sky-high. Josephine doesn't even bother to get dressed, let alone cook a meal. Mind you, she and Roger aren't married – perhaps that's the problem.'

'Well,' said Vanessa. 'Justin, please leave that alone.'

'Although she says he's a great help with the baby. These men! They're all fetching and carrying and changing nappies and doing the housework! Now that really is a big change. I'd love to know how their wives manage it, because we certainly never could. My husband thought the sky had fallen in if I asked him to put his own bread in the toaster! Mind you,' she added, onerously, 'I wonder whether some of these modern women might not come to regret it in the end. I wonder whether the – the *romance*,' she exclaimed, 'of marriage survives, once men and women have become so muddled up. Where's the privacy, the sense of mystery? Where's the excitement?'

Some time later, outside Mrs Daley's front door, which was closed, a fine rain began to fall. Vanessa stood in it with the two boys. The pram was gone; Vanessa had heard Mrs Daley call to her husband to move it, but she hadn't seen him. She had an impression of his immateriality, his silence. She wanted the pram back. She wanted to clean its wheels. She felt she had been breached, overrun. She set off with the boys back down the hill, carrying Danny in her arms. He struggled and writhed; he was heavy. After a few paces Justin said that he was tired and wanted her to carry him too. Mrs Daley, who had remarked at the door, looking at the rain, that it seemed like they should have come in the car after all, had not offered to drive them back herself. Vanessa hadn't expected her to: she was not surprised to encounter coldness, steel, in other women. Mrs Daley had put her out in the rain with two small children thinking –

quite rightly, Vanessa thought – that it was her own fault if that was how she found herself. Out on the lane, the sky darkened. A violent gust of wind blew up the hill and battered the leafless branches. The rain began to fall harder, and Vanessa saw that it would turn to a deluge, that they were twenty minutes, at Justin's pace, from home, and that in any case Justin was refusing to walk. Her hair was already drenched. Rain was running down Danny's face. Justin sat down in the road. This is what happens, thought Vanessa. This is what happens. She knew that she was about to cry. Some space inside her seemed to collapse. Her arms, holding Danny, felt weak. An ugly rictus, like a grin, spread across her face, hurting her cheeks.

'I'm going to walk off!' she said to Justin, and the strange sound of her voice made him start to bawl as he sat there in the road, and she saw that her frustration was pulling her and that the more she followed it the more everything would recede from her grasp. Yet she couldn't rein it back; she wanted to surrender to it, to feel it carry her bodily along. 'Get up!' she shouted. 'Get up!'

Danny bellowed and she heard herself telling him to shut up, to just shut up, and then she began to run in fury towards Justin through the rain, infused suddenly with strength, and at the sight of her he scrambled away on all fours shrieking. Just then the sound of a car horn caused her to turn. There was Serena Porter, with her window rolled down. She called at them to get in and then she got out of the car, leaving the engine running, and picked up Justin herself and put him on the back seat.

'That was lucky,' she said, when Vanessa got in beside her.

The rain pounded on the roof of the car. Water dripped

coldly from Vanessa's hair down her face and on to Danny, who sat like a stone on her lap. She looked behind her and saw Justin lying flat across the back seat with his head buried in his arms.

'Justin,' she said, reaching her hand back and touching his hair. He flinched and wriggled away from her.

'Ready?' said Serena, who was watching her with her hands on the steering wheel. She wore a sympathetic expression. Her hands were long and pale; a ring glittered on her finger. Vanessa could smell her perfume.

'He wouldn't walk,' said Vanessa.

'Oh!' sighed Serena, looking at the roof of the car. 'Isn't that the most infuriating thing?' She put the car in gear and they began to roll down the hill. 'They keep their legs crossed when you pick them up – I always feel like a policeman trying to move peace protesters out of the road.'

She laughed. Vanessa didn't believe her – she didn't believe that Serena knew how she felt. Serena, in that moment, seemed to carry about her the stamp of faraway places, like the girls you sometimes met working at travel agents or airports, all brown skin and vacant, pleasured eyes, all artificial sympathy for you, with your thousand bags and bawling children, your worried face on which no paradise would rub off, which threatened rather to dent, to despoil whatever it looked on.

'I lost my temper,' she said, because it was another prerequisite of these girls that you could not resist confessing to them your uglinesses.

'Oh, they'll forget it,' said Serena.

'Where are your children?'

'At home,' said Serena, looking askance at Vanessa with a smile. 'I gave them to Victor and made a run for it.'

'Where to?' said Vanessa, although she knew that it would hurt her to hear about Serena's little freedoms. 'Where have you been?'

'Town,' said Serena. 'What passes for town. I'll tell you what I did – I went to see a film.'

'Alone?'

Serena nodded. 'I haven't been to the cinema in the afternoon for years. I don't think I even really watched the film – I just sat there thinking, Nobody knows where I am. It was,' she added, leaning back in her seat, 'absolute bliss.'

Vanessa, trying to imagine this bliss, could get no sensation from it. She needed something stronger. She felt almost as though she would ask for it outright. She stared through the swimming windscreen at the blotchy grey prospect of the lane. As they rounded the corner her house appeared. It seemed to be leaning over; it looked derelict. It corresponded with her bleakly.

'Do you want a hand getting them in?' said Serena, stopping the car.

'No,' said Vanessa, 'I'm fine.'

For the second time that day – the first had been in Mrs Daley's kitchen – she felt an urgent need to escape. It was a need that arose from a sense of her own disorder. She looked at Serena's legs, in jeans, next to her on the seat, at her long red hair. In that moment there seemed to be nothing companionable in the world. Vanessa got out of the car with Danny and opened the back door. Justin still lay there across the seat.

'Come on,' she said.

'I want to stay here,' said Justin.

'Come on, get out.'

'No!'

She grabbed his wrist and hauled him bellowing out of the car and into the rain. She needed to get into the house. It was an admission of defeat, like climbing into comfortable, dreary clothes. She wanted to expand into that dreariness, to sink from view. She toiled up the path, Danny writhing on her hip, Justin dragging his legs so that he made great skips in the air when she pulled him up. At the door she turned, as if to wave, and saw that Serena had already gone.

The house was dark, its rooms cold and slate-grey; Colin wasn't there. Vanessa put the boys in front of the television and went and sat alone in the kitchen. She had a desire to make peace with them, but she couldn't quite find her way to realising it. It was as though having the desire were enough. Thinking of herself on the lane, shouting as if she were mad, she felt ashamed. It left her with nothing – it demolished at a stroke her sense of a hierarchy. Already, her thoughts about Colin had overrun the place of detention. This was not an unpleasant sensation; it gave her the hit she was looking for. Sitting at the kitchen table, her mind hovered over everything, exalted and benign. She found that she didn't care that Serena had witnessed her behaviour in the lane. She stood up to switch on the lights and then sat down again. It seemed that if she switched on the lights this position might change; she would care, about everything. Rain dripped methodically from her coat on to the floor. In the room, the grey light deepened, so that everything acquired density and became like things not seen but remembered, lacking the animation of light. Here was her habitat: her mind dwelled in it, rudimentary, pulsing, alive. How could she be at once so sheltered and so estranged? The world seemed to her to be full of indifference. It was a blank: it was ungoverned, it was without morality. You dug and tended your corner of it – this, she realised, was why she found Serena Porter ridiculous. She pretended that things were other than they were. Vanessa, the only woman in a house of males, felt that she carried within her the germ of civilisation, like a missionary in a savage place. If she got sick, it was not a sickness of conviction – it was a mere, temporary recrudescence of the facts. She thought of Serena, sitting alone in the provincial cinema in the middle of the afternoon, and nearly laughed. Was that it? Was that all Vanessa had to be afraid of? Next time she was in town she would buy the newspaper Serena wrote for. With her every thought in print, Vanessa reflected, Serena had a limited ability to conceal herself.

Passing through the sitting room on her way upstairs to change her clothes, she was confronted by the spectacle of the boys, still in their wet coats, staring at the flickering television through the gloom. They seemed distant. They didn't seem to care, about anything. She wanted to pick them up and clasp them to her and infuse them with withheld love; to secure them, against whatever losses the future might hold.

Serena's column was not quite what Vanessa was expecting. She bought the newspaper on three consecutive days before she found it, half a page entitled 'Life Lines' and headed by a small photograph of Serena smiling knowingly, with her hair arranged over her shoulders. There wasn't much in it about sexual equality, as far as Vanessa could see. It was all about Serena and her children. Vanessa was startled to notice that she used their real names. These children corresponded strangely with the real children, the children

Vanessa had met. Serena was writing about her recent attempt to take her daughters for a walk in the countryside. Some way into this account, Vanessa realised that Serena was describing her own predicament on the lane, when it had started to rain and she had lost her temper with Justin and Danny. Quickly she read it through to the end. The whole story was made to seem very humorous, even the part in which Serena claimed to have raged at her children as they sat there in the wet road. Vanessa supposed that it would seem funny, if it hadn't happened to you.

It all added to the feeling she had now, of life moving in a stately, silent procession away from her, so that everything familiar seemed to look on her with a baleful expression of farewell. Her husband, her children, the rooms of her house were revealing themselves to her in a valedictory pageant. Colin had secured a loan against the house: they were in crisis, but Vanessa knew rather than felt this fact. She viewed Colin not from within the circle of a shared predicament but from a distance, as though he was enacting his tragedy on a stage and she, in the audience, was weeping tears of pity for him. She pitied her children even more. Her brain was besieged by the sense of an ending, and it had transposed her love into a minor key: she saw her children as orphaned, and she pitied them with all her heart. She saw herself, quite clearly, dying, a death that was already under way, a death from causes that she could identify only as her own ambivalence, her doubt. She had recently telephoned three employment agencies in town and made appointments. All of them asked her what she could do and she had nearly laughed, because she felt as though she could do anything; that there was nothing so hard, in the world beyond her house – a world that seemed to her to be full of choices and soft surfaces, of pretence, of bloodless illusion – nothing so hard as her life, which had created other lives, and which rested in her core like coal, a seam, a rich unavailing density.

It was December now. The decayed mantle of summer had fallen from the village: a whole epoch of industry and fruition had yellowed and broken down and been shed, as it seemed to Vanessa, without regret. Now the houses stood unadorned in the pale flat light of winter. An invitation had arrived, as it did every year, for the Daleys' Christmas drinks, and Vanessa placed it on the mantelpiece in the sitting room, from where it looked at her as she came and went, through day after difficult day, until it too acquired an aspect of finality, as though it were the invitation to a fate that had been not avoided but temporarily deferred.

'I couldn't find you in the paper,' said Vanessa. 'I looked, and they'd put something else on your page.'

'They've moved me to Saturdays,' said Serena.

'Oh,' said Vanessa. 'I thought you might have given it up.'

'Given up what?' Serena laughed. 'The struggle?'

'I liked what you wrote.'

'Well, I'm still there. I've just been redesigned. Twice the number of words.'

'But not twice the money, I suppose.'

Vanessa chiselled at the raw flesh of a potato with a knife until the shape of a Christmas tree stood out on it. The children sat at the other end of the table with their paper and paints, waiting. Her fingers holding the knife looked red and sore, and she had a sense of herself painfully guiding them all through one moment and then the next, like a needle pulling a thread through cloth.

'We'll use sponges next time,' she said. 'They're more expensive but they're a lot quicker. Sorry,' she added. 'I've become very boring about money.' She leaned across the table and moved a pot of paint away from Justin's elbow. 'Colin thinks we should just cancel Christmas this year. Well, to be more precise he said that if I wanted to spend money on all that rubbish I'd have to go out and earn it myself.'

She felt the blood rushing to her face and so she took another potato from the bag and bent her head over it.

'You could hardly be called extravagant,' said Serena, 'for going to town on a few sponges. Anyway, I'm sure something will come up.'

'It has to,' said Vanessa emphatically. 'Because there's nothing else. You'd be surprised how many people have money from other sources – you know, family money, trust funds, stocks and shares. They can afford to take time off. We can't. I'm lucky,' she concluded. 'I've just got the children to worry about.' Colin had made more or less exactly this speech to her the previous evening. 'But it's the division,' she continued. 'It's his saying, This is mine and if you want something you have to go out and get it for yourself. But you don't get paid for doing housework.'

'There are people who think that you should,' said Serena.

'That's ridiculous,' said Vanessa.

'I think they mean it symbolically,' said Serena. 'A form of public acknowledgement.'

'Some people are lucky,' said Vanessa. 'They never get to this point. There's always plenty of money and they never have to think about whose it actually is. But Colin, he's all my house, my car, my table, even my children, except when it comes to looking after them,' she added, lowering her voice. 'I suppose he's no different from any other man. I don't want to be one of those women who just sits there moaning about how they're all the same, but in some respects they are. Colin's pretty good really,' she concluded matter-of-factly. 'He's just under a lot of pressure.'

'So are you,' suggested Serena.

'I'd hardly call this –' she held up a potato – 'high pressure.'

'Pressure of a different sort,' said Serena.

'Sometimes,' said Vanessa presently, 'I think that I'm the selfish one. I want to have it both ways.'

'In what sense? You know,' she added, when Vanessa failed to reply, 'I've found our conversations very interesting. In fact, I've used them in my column.'

'I know,' said Vanessa.

'Do you? And there was I thinking I'd disguised it so well.'

'I don't mind.'

'It's strange,' said Serena, putting her elbows on the table and resting her chin on her hands. 'For a long time I was so angry.'

'What were you angry about?'

Serena shrugged.

'Men. Marriage. Children. I don't know, everything.' She smiled. 'People don't like angry women. They think it's ugly. It spoils their fun. Sometimes it would take me an hour to write a single line. When I was a child,' she said, 'I used to have to try really hard to make myself cry. That was what writing was like for me. And now it's the opposite. It's so easy that I can hardly bring myself to stop.'

'You're doing well for yourself,' said Vanessa sourly.

'And all that happened,' mused Serena, 'was that I finally worked out that people prefer what's true to what's right. Even if the truth is that they're powerless. Women, I mean. I don't think I knew what women were actually like. I only knew what I was like, and that I couldn't have lived their lives for one day. The funny thing is,' she said, 'that I liked men more when I was angry with them.'

Serena's thin body, clad entirely in black, seemed to vibrate beside Vanessa's with a strange tension. She extended her pale hand with a frantic clinking of gold bracelets and placed it on Vanessa's arm. Vanessa felt large and stolid. Her skin did not receive the sensation of Serena's hand; it was as though Serena had placed her hand on the arm of an overstuffed chair.

'We're going through a difficult time here as well,' said Serena, in a rapid voice that was like the broken shards of something that had fallen to the floor. 'I can't talk about it now. I'll tell you another time.'

Vanessa saw the flash of water in Serena's narrow black eyes. Her lids and eyelashes were clogged with make-up and the tears cleaved to it brightly before Serena blinked them away.

Standing at her kitchen window, Vanessa was surprised to see Victor out in the lane. He was standing completely still beside their front gate, with his back to the house. He reached an arm behind him and laid it on the wooden fence. Vanessa could see his breath coming out in misty puffs that dispersed slowly into the pale, cold afternoon. He stood there for some minutes, as though struck by a great thought. When it seemed he wasn't going to move, Vanessa left the children inside and went out to invite him into the house.

'Home seemed very far away just then,' he said, following her slowly up the path.

Looking at him, Vanessa realised that he was ill. He was often in London when she visited Serena, and she hadn't seen him for a few weeks. He had lost weight. The kitchen, where they were sitting, was full of cold light in which Victor's face looked glacial, blue-white around its protuberances of bone, its animus close to the skin. His eyes were forlorn and excited and ringed with shadow. He had kept on his coat, from which the intricacy of his knotty hands and throat and his thin legs protruded. He seemed to Vanessa fragile and expressive, like a child or a work of art. He wore a brown knitted hat on his head which framed the shock of his face. Vanessa opened her mouth to speak and at that moment Colin emerged from his study.

'Hello?' he said, in an affronted voice, as though Victor were an intruder whom Vanessa had for some reason not noticed.

'This is Victor Porter,' said Vanessa. 'This is my husband, Colin.'

'Ah!' said Colin, bearing down on Victor with his hand outstretched. 'The great man – at last we meet!'

Vanessa turned away before she could see their hands touch. Danny and Justin were sitting on the floor playing with their train set, which lay around them in pieces like a disaster. She watched her children as they investigated the sections of track, the little wooden carriages. Justin was mumbling to himself. Danny held a signal box in the clamp of his fingers, which occasionally he raised to his mouth. To Vanessa they seemed as though in the foothills of a towering comprehension: they were so patient, the way they did the work of studying the world. She watched their small busy hands and thought of how she had witnessed those hands, those bodies, acquiring their competence. For hour after hour she had presided over their formation, so that it seemed to her that her children remained her creation even though her body no longer possessed them. There was very little about them that was strange to her. She believed she could almost see into their minds, the way a jeweller could lift the back off a watch with a special key and see into the pulsing mechanism.

'– nice for her to have another mum in the village,' said Colin.

She put the kettle on and started to make tea. The men sitting at the table seemed suddenly much larger than her and somehow elevated, as though, like her sons, she saw everything at ankle-height. The water stirred and rasped in the kettle.

'– market for documentary films is non-existent. I can't afford to make them any more. I love the work but it's like having children – nice, but it doesn't put food on the table.'

She placed a cup beside Victor's white hand. The heavy china and the scalding liquid looked strangely threatening. He made no move to pick it up. Instead he folded his arms across his chest as though to protect himself.

'I can see that,' he said.

'For instance,' said Colin, 'I made a film a few years ago that I would never find a buyer for today. It would be seen as too risky. Yet at the time it was one of the channel's big success stories.'

'I don't suppose,' said Victor, 'that I could have some sugar?'

'That's not really my department,' said Colin, raising his hands palms-up. 'Vanessa?'

'I'll get some.'

'What was it about?' said Victor. 'Your film.'

'It was about cricket teas. No, don't laugh,' Colin said gaily. 'It was sort of my pet subject, you know, remnants of a vanished England, little pieces of the past. Things we've lost our respect for. I'd always wanted to make a film about cricket –' he leaned forwards confidentially – 'but one day I thought, Hey, why not make it from the female point of view? So the men are these blurred white figures in the background, and instead we're inside, in the pavilion, in a world where the thickness of the cucumber in the sandwiches is a matter of life and death. Tells you something about the difference between the sexes, doesn't it?' He paused. 'And the thing was, people *loved* it.'

'I don't think you'd get away with it now,' said Vanessa. 'I think things have changed.'

'There you are,' said Colin bitterly. 'They say it's the housewives that make or break a programme.'

'Women want to be taken more seriously,' said Vanessa.

'I'll just leave you to run the company, then, shall I? Is that serious enough for you?'

Victor rose from his chair.

'Thank you,' he said. 'I must be on my way.'

Vanessa saw him to the door and watched him go down the path.

'He wasn't entirely with it,' said Colin when he'd gone. 'I saw him on telly once talking about some case or other. You'd never know it was him. If you ask me, that woman's worn him out.'

*

Vanessa found out about Victor from Serena's column. She didn't always read it – it embarrassed her slightly now, as though by reading it she were prying into Serena's private thoughts, although of course it was the other way around. She wondered sometimes whether Victor felt the same thing. It seemed to her that Serena's actual life and the life she described in her column were separate. Vanessa found it difficult to guess Serena's feelings when she met her face to face. In the messy kitchen in the big pink house Serena's behaviour was formless, almost expectant, as though a day were nothing more than a disordered collection of facts over which she would hover until something glinted and caught her eye. Vanessa imagined Serena's mind to be like the nest of some thieving clever bird, lined with stolen fragments.

Yet reading about Victor, standing in her coat in the cold car park of the supermarket where she had just spent a furtive hour, she was filled with the sense not of Serena's opportunism nor of her tragedy, but of her strangeness. It was not the awful disclosure itself but everything that had preceded it that now struck Vanessa as strange. She and Victor must have known about his illness for months – that was the reason, she supposed, they had moved down to Ravenley. For all that time, week in and week out, Serena had written as though in ignorance of this terrible fact. She had written things which could only have caused her pain; things which, in the light of Victor's predicament, appeared to Vanessa more fabricated even than she knew them to be. She glanced automatically through the car window at the children, who were sitting on the back seat waiting for her to get in; and seeing her own reflection in the glass a feeling of sorrow struck her chest. She let it pass through her.

There had been a time, when she was younger, when a feeling such as this would have taken hold of her whole body; but now emotion travelled through her as through a tunnel, or a corridor at the centre of a great building, leaving the rest of her untouched. She had a sense of herself as that building, compartmentalised, lit up, indifferent. She got in the car and drove back to Ravenley, remembering that she had felt sad about Victor, and wondering whether this sadness would visit her again.

In the third week of December it turned cold. Night after night hard frosts petrified the village so that in the morning the grass was stiff and white and basins of ice formed in the potholes in the road. The days were brief and pale and it got dark at four o'clock. Vanessa bought a small Christmas tree and put it up in the sitting room, where she and the boys hung it with last year's decorations. In the evenings she put on her coat and went out to the freezing garage, where she was making a playhouse out of old bits of wood to give to the boys as their Christmas present. It wasn't very good but she knew they wouldn't mind – they were too small to know the difference. It was she who minded. One evening she drove a nail into her thumb and the pain was so great that it was all she could do to stagger back across the still black yard to the house and up the stairs to her bed. She bound it up tightly with a handkerchief and passed out, still clothed, on top of the covers. When she woke some hours later, stiff with cold and her eyes full of electric light, she saw her hand lying beside her like the hand of someone dead, in a great delta of blood. It had soaked all the way through to the mattress. She changed the covers and turned the mattress over so that Colin wouldn't find out.

But in fact Colin never went into their bedroom any more. He was hardly at home at all. He stayed out all day, and late at night came back so silently that Vanessa only knew he had slept there by the fact that the door to the spare room was closed in the morning. She and the boys were usually having breakfast when he passed through the kitchen, and although he always spoke to his sons and kissed them, he showed Vanessa only the white, wordless slab of his face on his way out. He behaved as though she had done something to offend him, but she knew from her children's moods that he was just playing to her as to the audience of his disaffection. Nevertheless, she found herself unable to broach with him its actual cause. For the six years of their marriage she had been a bystander in the matter of money. It was hard not to feel, in the presence of his rude silences and broad, perennially turned back, that Colin had begun to ruminate on this fact; that he regarded Vanessa and the children as a luxury that had stealthily and bindingly become a burden. In his ceaseless comings and goings she heard the silent accusation of her own stolidity. It was true that she had not followed up her interview with the employment agency in town, where she had learned what her dormant secretarial skills could earn her. Once she'd subtracted the cost of paying someone to look after the children, the sum that was left had not struck Vanessa as a sufficient price for leaving them. She had not disclosed this sum to Colin: she suspected that he would not agree. No amount of money, as far as he was concerned, could be under the present circumstances too small. Privately, Vanessa was glad that it was so small – it helped her to conceal from herself the fact that in this storm of their marriage it was the children and not Colin whom her instincts told her to save, and that in the matter of their care she could not be bribed nor even driven from them by necessity. Colin couldn't have it both ways. He had liked her dependence when it had suited him. Vanessa had been Colin's secretary, in the job he had had before he'd set up on his own. In those days he had scorned the women who had fought him for his place in the world. If he'd wanted a woman like that he should have married one. She remembered what those women used to say about Colin in her hearing, and then, she supposed, out of it once the fact of their relationship became known around the office.

Her hand felt as though it had turned to lead: a hard, heavy ache lived there night and day. The pain was a sort of penance. She painted the playhouse with her other hand and it looked like the work of a child, heartbreaking and hopeful, impermanent.

Serena wanted holly, and Vanessa knew where it grew in big unruly bushes, along a path at the edge of the village. They took the children down there one afternoon. She didn't mind going, in spite of the fact that her hand hurt and her eyes burned with the tiredness of being kept awake by it. It was four days to Christmas, but Vanessa believed that those days would never pass; some blockage had jammed the wheels of time and left the future drifting, inaccessible, as though it lay on the far side of a body of water and could be seen but not reached. On Thursday they were due to go to the Daleys' party. She and Colin went to the Daleys' every year: this fact, like the fact of Christmas itself, was immutable, and yet it seemed to Vanessa that both events would only occur once things between herself and Colin had been put right.

In the kitchen of the pink house she had found Serena beneath a pall of smoke. A strong smell of burning hung in the air. Serena was ladling mincemeat clumsily into pastry cases while Margret and Frances sat crying at her feet. Now, walking along the frozen lane, her breath coming out in white spurts, she was talking rapidly about garlands and how she planned to hang the holly in loops around the table for Christmas lunch, as she had seen it done in a magazine.

'That might be a bit uncomfortable,' said Vanessa, 'if it was right in your lap.'

Serena was walking too quickly for her. She stalked ahead, thin and frantic, with Margret wailing at her heels.

'I hadn't thought of that,' she said, stopping abruptly and then setting off again. 'Oh well, we'll just have to sit well back.'

Vanessa was pushing Danny's chair with one hand while the other was in her pocket. Justin plodded silently along beside her. Lately she had felt an awareness, a sort of consternation, beginning to rise from her elder son. It was being drawn towards her, inadvertently, like a plant towards a source of light. They turned off the lane and went down the path, where the earth stood in hard ridges under-foot. Serena cried out at the sight of the holly bushes and immediately set to work cutting branches.

'Look!' she said to Margret, who had wrapped both her arms around her mother's leg and was sobbing with her face pressed against her trousers. 'Look, isn't this fun!'

Margret didn't look. She mashed her face against the cloth and trampled the ground with her feet. Justin picked up a stick and began to beat it against the rustling body of a bush. The branches quivered. Vanessa turned away from him and bent to where Danny sat in his chair to pull his hat down over his ears. Just then, the sound of a voice came clearly through the still air from behind the row of conifers that stood on the other side of the path.

'Pick it up.'

It was a man's voice, elderly and well-spoken. The voice was so close and so unexpected that Vanessa and Serena were both startled and turned around.

'No, I won't pick it up,' said a woman's voice.

'That's my brand-new –' a sob from Margret obscured the word – 'asked you to take care of it and you've left it lying on the ground.'

'Pick it up yourself,' said the woman.

Vanessa and Serena looked at each other. Justin stood still with his stick raised in his hand.

'I hate you,' said the man, after a silence. 'I've always hated you.'

'Oh, have you now!' laughed the woman.

'Yes,' said the man stubbornly. 'You've taken my soul away.'

'Of all the excuses I've ever heard—'

Margret had stopped crying and was listening. Serena bent down and placed her hands over her daughter's ears.

'– do you think you've taken from me?' said the woman. She swore, one obscenity after another, and then emitted a preternatural squawk. The man gave out a high-pitched moan.

'Who is it?' whispered Serena.

'It must be the Brownings,' said Vanessa, plotting in her mind which of the houses that faced the lane the voices were coming from.

'Who are they?'

'They're retired,' said Vanessa. 'They're on the church committee.'

'That should fix it,' said the man just then. He spoke in a voice that was flat but perfectly friendly.

'Oh yes,' said the woman. 'I should think so.'

'It was the frost,' said the man. 'You don't expect it this early—'

The voices got fainter and then disappeared. Then came the sound of a door closing. Serena stood there on the path with a stricken expression on her face.

'How horrible,' she said.

'What were they talking about?' asked Justin.

'Nothing,' said Vanessa.

'How violent,' said Serena.

The light was failing. A strange blue tint lay over the fields. The land looked helpless as it awaited the dark. Vanessa quickly helped Serena fill her basket and they turned back towards the house.

'I never heard my parents argue,' said Serena. 'Not once.'

'You were lucky,' said Vanessa.

'When my mother left my father lay on the sofa and cried. I remember going in when it got dark and putting a blanket over him.'

'Why did she leave?' said Vanessa.

'She wanted to be on her own.' Serena shrugged. 'It was exactly this time of year, nearly Christmas, and no one had bought a tree or got any presents. They just forgot about it, I suppose. So all through Christmas Day I just sat there with my father, desperate to tell him what day it was but not daring to. He still loves her, even now. When she left he became a sort of child that we had to look after.'

They reached the lane. The village lay as though under water, silent, lightless, except for the pale-orange squares of windows whose curtains had already been drawn. Staring at the dark unpeopled vista, Serena sighed.

'I never thought I'd be somewhere like this,' she said. 'Trying to make everything all right. Except it isn't all right, even here. There's no more love here than anywhere else.'

'Why should there be?' said Vanessa.

'Oh, I don't know. Because people don't think so much. Because they don't believe in things that will set them apart. You know, I've been a bad person in many ways and Victor has forgiven it all, he's never held me to ransom for any of it, and yet now, of all times—'

'Mummy,' said Justin, 'I'm cold.'

Vanessa bent and picked up her son and wrapped him in her coat.

'What have you done to your hand?' said Serena.

'Oh, it's nothing.'

'Let's get back to the house,' said Serena. 'It's freezing.'

'I love her,' said Colin.

He said it with his arms folded, leaning back against the kitchen dresser. Vanessa stared at the bulge of his stomach beneath his black polo-neck sweater, his broad denimed haunches. The kitchen seemed dense and cluttered with evening, exiguous, striped with shadow and electric light.

'Don't be ridiculous,' she said.

'I *love* her,' said Colin. His tongue got in the way of his need to emphasise this point: saliva foamed minutely at the corners of his mouth.

'Well, what do you expect me to do about it?'

Colin tilted his head back and thrust the sharp point of

his nose into the air. His eyes were half-closed. He seemed to be trying to catch some scent, some nuance from the air: a whiff of inspiration in the strong, unventilated atmosphere of Vanessa. He lowered his head and expelled his breath in a long, whistling sigh.

'Let me go,' he said, opening his eyes wide.

He was looking at her, or at a point very near her. When it settled on her his gaze seemed to slip slightly to one side, as though there were nothing in her to get a grip on.

'Please,' she said. 'Please, Colin.'

'I've done this –' he gestured irritably with his hands, whirling them around his ears – 'this thing. This family thing. Six years. *Six years*,' he repeated, as if to amaze her. 'It's a long time, Vanessa. I'm dying. I feel – like – I'm *dying*.' He thumped on the wooden countertop, for emphasis.

'What's her name?' said Vanessa. 'Actually, I don't want to know. Don't tell me.'

'Lorraine,' said Colin, as he might have said 'nothing'.

'Is she married?'

'Was. Was. She got out.' He bit his lip and tilted his head back again.

'Children?'

Colin shook his head, slowly, from side to side.

'And what about our children?' said Vanessa.

'Don't,' said Colin, holding his hand out like a policeman, 'start.'

'Does she know that you don't have any money?' said Vanessa presently.

'She's got her own money,' said Colin. He couldn't stop himself from sounding proud. 'She runs her own company. She's very successful.'

'But if you leave, you'll still have to pay for our support.'

'Details,' said Colin, whirling his hands around his ears again.

'How will you manage to do that?'

'This isn't about money,' said Colin loudly. 'I'll sell the house if I have to,' he added, after a while. His skin was very white, the disingenuous, simple white of some obscure Celtic ancestry on which the modern scheme of his personality seemed in that moment superimposed.

'You can't,' said Vanessa.

'Why not?'

'Because – because I don't choose it.'

'It's my house,' said Colin.

'Am I completely insignificant?' said Vanessa.

'Don't,' said Colin.

'Please answer my question. Am I?'

Colin folded his arms again and turned his head away. Vanessa left the kitchen and went upstairs. Quickly she checked the children in their beds and then withdrew to her room, shutting the door behind her. It was cold; it would freeze again tonight. She got into bed without taking off her clothes and pulled the covers over her head.

Unexpectedly, she fell straight into a black, featureless sleep. When she opened her eyes again the room was full of grey, powdery light. She had forgotten to draw the curtains. She got up immediately. A strange, prescient hush drew her to the window. Looking out, she saw snow. Everything had been erased, the raw, painful detail of the garden, the jagged silhouettes of trees, the sharp-edged, crushed-metal ugliness of winter, all gone. The whole etiolated prospect was obliterated by a thick carpet of white. Vanessa stood at the window. Presently she went out into the hall. The children remained silent in their beds. The door to the spare room was shut; Colin was still here. She moved noiselessly down the stairs and into the kitchen. It was seven o'clock. The boys would wake up at any moment. She put on her coat and let herself out of the front door.

The sky, having shed its burden of snow, was pale and effaced. Everything was quiet. Vanessa stood on the muffled lane and wondered whether she was dreaming: the white, noiseless landscape seemed like the landscape of her own mind. Some acknowledgement of her appeared to lie in this fact, the acknowledgement of a mysterious authority. It expressed the view, this authority, that nature had been affronted in the person of Vanessa, and that its wrath would be generous. It interested her, the idea that a wound to the heart could bring forth an effusion of beauty, ice-cold, ravishing, melting in the hand; that she could be pierced to the core and merely reveal deeper and deeper reserves of graciousness. She set off with her hands in her pockets. The valley was completely silent. Her boots sank softly. There was no one else about. She felt as though every property of her life had fallen away and she moved in her own element, in her memories, in the particular cadences of her being. The man, the two children and the house lay behind her, like stones in the middle of a stream that flowed on, travelling between white crusted banks, liquid, animated, senseless. She walked slowly, across the field behind the church and up to the top of the hill. Turning around she saw the track of her footprints ascending behind her. She wished those marks could be erased. She felt decided and firm and yet the desire to be ethereal, to stop, to cease, balked at that decision, so that she was estranged from herself, mutually hostile, at war. She had to live, but her feelings were rebelling against the living. They wanted to go their own way. This was a situation that would split her in two. She grasped inside herself for a common aim – her children. One day her children would leave her too, but that didn't matter, it was so far away in time that some geological process seemed to lie between then and now, the years of her ageing, of her formation. She would be a different person, evolved to future conditions. Going back down, she saw a small figure in the snow on the opposite side of the valley. It was a man and he was waving his arm. She recognised it as Victor and she waved back, smiling, even though he couldn't possibly see her face.

Colin was sitting at the kitchen table in his dressing gown. His hair stood on end. Vanessa could hear the sound of the television in the next-door room. He looked up when she came in, his mouth open.

'Are the roads blocked?' he said.

'Yes,' said Vanessa. 'You're stuck here today, I'm afraid.'

Colin did not reply. She felt him staring at her as she made herself a cup of coffee. She took it upstairs and stood on the landing, not moving. She heard Danny crying and then, after a while, the heavy scrape of Colin's chair. Shortly afterwards there were clattering sounds, and more crying, and the indistinct, severe bass of Colin's voice.

'I'm hungry,' said Justin. 'Dad, I'm hungry. I'm hungry, Da—'

'Shut up,' said Colin. 'For Christ's sake.'

The siren of Justin's cry made Vanessa lean her head against the wall. Tears flowed from her eyes, hot and profuse, and dripped on to the carpet. She went into the bathroom and locked the door. She sat on the edge of the bath with the taps turned on and after a long time she got into the water. Her body, white, squarish, anomalous, seemed huge and strangely untouched. It was her head that was plagued; the drama concentrated itself there, noisy, interminable, maddeningly compacted. She felt as though she were a passenger in a car going too fast: her mind strained with the consciousness of danger, but there was no pain, and because she felt nothing physical she kept drifting towards indifference. Her hand, bruised and purplish, floated numbly in the water beside her. The injury made more sense to her now, in view of her conversation with Colin. It was her actual wound; it was a sign. She got out and stood by the window brushing her long hair. The snow was already tarnished by the dull, late-morning light. The noises had stopped downstairs. The boys' absence boomed around her. It was better not to know what was going on. There wasn't much they could do to hurt themselves inside, and if Colin had taken them out then cold was the only problem. She guessed that Colin would let them get far from the house, and at that furthest point their ability to manage would promptly expire. She had learned to eke out this quality, their tolerance, to within seconds. She could contain them in time; she'd had to, because they had no sense of time themselves. They never knew what the next minute would bring them. Their requirements, to them, were unforecast. This was her genius, her skill, the management of time. Alone, she felt both ennobled and isolated by this peculiar qualification. It seemed that she was the only person who did not desire what she couldn't have. Her competence accounted for everything: there was nothing inside her that was beyond her control. The idea, for example, of falling in love – she could entertain this idea, but she couldn't ever see it becoming more than that, even if she'd wanted it to. And it didn't mean that much, that

Colin claimed to have fallen in love: it was in the practical consequences of this claim that the substance lay. The insult came not in the person of this woman, whom she vaguely imagined to be exactly like Colin, but in Colin's inability to see by what she, Vanessa, would be affronted. Recondite, institutional, the opposite of vain – she wasn't going to take offence over issues of love, or even fidelity. No, it was the question of significance that mattered. She had no proof that she was significant – she had never asked for proof, from anybody – but she was, she knew she was. She curated the right things; she managed time; she was in contact with life at the highest levels: she was important.

She went downstairs to the kitchen, which was empty. Half-eaten bowls of cereal stood on the table. Through the window she saw that the car was still there. She put on her coat and went out, at one minute believing that she was going in search of her husband and children and at the next that she was escaping the trap of the house before Colin had the chance to come back and close the door on it. She walked down the road feeling strangely weightless. She hadn't been alone in the day for years, not since before Justin was born. Her boots squeaked in the snow. Out of habit she turned up the lane towards the pink house and went through the gate. In the snow the house looked buried and uninhabited and Vanessa guessed that Serena wasn't there, but she knocked at the door and waited and after a long time, in which there was only silence, it opened. It was Victor who opened it. He looked at Vanessa as if he didn't recognise her and she too was surprised, not only because she was expecting Serena but because when she went to houses it was always to see women, and there was some familiarity of form, some bodily recognition, an exchange of needs, that stopped you ever really looking or asking yourself why you had come. Vanessa asked herself this now.

'I'm sorry to turn up on your doorstep,' she said, turning as if to go. 'I'm sure you're busy. I was just passing by.'

'Come in,' he said. He stood back and opened the door wider. 'Come in out of the cold.'

Inside the rooms were warm and pensive, full of gathered air. Vanessa knew immediately that Serena and the children weren't there. She followed Victor into the kitchen. It was very neat. Its orderly appearance seemed to be the expression of Victor, his compact maleness, his mastery of facts. A woman's presence was more spreading, it flowed around things and encompassed them and made everything the same. Vanessa felt a sort of rigour impose itself between herself and her feelings about Colin. This was a pleasing sensation: it suggested the possibility of things remaining within her control. Victor looked better than he had the last time she'd seen him. There was colour in his face. He was wearing his brown hat and what looked like several jumpers, one on top of the other.

'I'll make some tea,' he said. 'Was that you this morning, out on the hill?'

'Yes.'

'It was like a dream, wasn't it? It reminded me of being a child,' said Victor. 'Not that my childhood was spent anywhere as salubrious as this. But the world turning white, and all being well.'

'I don't think it's like that for them,' said Vanessa. 'They don't know.'

Victor slowly opened a cupboard and took out two cups.

'Don't know what?' he said. 'That the world's such a horrible place? I think I always knew that. I imbibed it with my mother's milk. My mistake was to think that I could do something about it.'

He shuffled to and fro in his slippered feet.

'I try to understand things for them,' said Vanessa, 'as a way of understanding them myself. Sometimes,' she said, 'I think that if it wasn't for the children I wouldn't exist.'

Victor paused, holding the dry disc of a teabag in his fingers.

'I felt that about the law,' he said. 'When I got ill people kept telling me how dispensable I was to try and make me feel better.'

'But wasn't that partly true?'

'Not really. The law is just an instrument. It's all,' he said, 'in the interpretation.'

'There must be other people, though.'

'You mean, people who are better?'

'Who are the same.'

'Maybe there are,' said Victor. 'But that doesn't help me. Any more than knowing that there are other mothers of other children would help you. To leave them, that is.'

'It would make it worse,' said Vanessa.

'Even a child,' said Victor, 'is not entirely your creation. Not the way a case is. I don't worry about my children half as much as I worry about my clients. Which I'm sure some people,' he added, 'would find despicable.'

'What do you mean?' said Vanessa.

'Just that we have so many rules about love,' he said.

'In that case I'm despicable too,' said Vanessa with a small smile.

'Because what tortures me,' continued Victor, 'what keeps

me awake at night is knowing that someone's in prison who shouldn't be there. And knowing that the reason for it is that I didn't have enough time.'

'Who is it?'

'What?'

'The person you mentioned.'

'Well,' said Victor, 'there is one. She's in a prison not far from here, actually.'

'What did she do?'

'They said she killed a woman and her two children. She set fire to their house.'

'How awful,' said Vanessa. She saw the house, the red branches of fire, and the woman, who seemed to be Vanessa herself, flanked by the small silhouettes of her children. 'But it wasn't true?'

'No.'

He brought the cups to the table and sat down. In his chair he looked light and jointed, as though he could be folded smaller and smaller until he disappeared.

'How did you know?'

'I didn't know for certain. It was becoming clear.' He raised his cup to his pale, papery lips. 'And now it's all sitting in a file somewhere gathering dust.'

'Do you go and see her? You said she wasn't far from here.'

'No,' said Victor. 'There's nothing I can do for her. I tried to refer her to someone I knew but she wasn't interested. She gave up hope.'

'But that wasn't your fault.'

Victor sighed.

'Well, it was really. I was in hospital for a few weeks last year and I gave the case to my assistant. She messed it up.

Kirsty was pregnant and the baby got taken into care. That was not,' he said, 'the plan.'

'What about Serena? Couldn't she do something?'

Victor laughed.

'Like what? Bake a cake and take it round? That's not really her line.'

'Write something,' said Vanessa. 'In the newspaper.'

'Serena's quite hard-hearted,' said Victor. 'She thinks people like Kirsty are ten a penny. Or rather, she refuses to be incapacitated by the thought that there might be a thousand Kirstys. I think she thinks that once she started caring she wouldn't be able to stop. She used to take an interest,' he added, turning and looking out at the white, laden garden as though he expected to see Serena coming up the path. 'In her firebrand days. But now she only wants to think about nice things.'

'I suppose we all do,' said Vanessa.

'I suppose so,' said Victor. He looked around him as though he'd lost something. 'Where are your children?'

'I left them with Colin,' said Vanessa. 'And made a run for it.'

'That's good,' said Victor. 'That must be very pleasant.'

When she stood up to leave Victor followed her out of the front door and into the garden, where the snow had sculpted everything into obscure, feminine forms that stretched sleepily away into the distance. For a moment, looking at the quiet village before she trod down the lane that would show her her own house, Vanessa felt exhilaration. It seemed to stem from an idea she suddenly had, that when she rounded that bend her house would not be there; that she was free eternally to inhabit this moment, which, unlike other moments, did not appear to contain anything to hurt her. She glanced at Victor and saw in profile his pouchy face with its ridges of bone, the brown scrub of his hair. He seemed all at once complicated and very far away from her: she couldn't imagine how he could be reached. The broad tub of Colin's body, the cast of his mind, had moulded her so that when she looked at another man she saw only jarring surfaces and things that didn't fit; and he too, Victor, bore Serena's impression, he was like an empty shoe standing there, worn, expectant, temporarily defunct.

'It's been nice to talk,' said Victor, and he smiled a ghastly smile that caused a shadow to pass over Vanessa's heart.

Colin wouldn't say if he was going to the Daleys' party. He lay on the sofa in his jeans watching television, observing an infinite silence. Vanessa had organised a babysitter to come at six. Because he refused to speak to her, there were other things she didn't know: whether, for example, Colin planned to leave her and when, or whether in fact he believed he already had. His silence was full of reproaches. Did he accuse Vanessa of blocking his path to the door and the shadowy life that lay beyond it? She had not asked him to leave, but as his wife she felt entitled to her reticence. She had planned on assuming the solid, unprovoking stance of a piece of furniture. This, it appeared, was Colin's plan also. She wondered whether he was waiting for her to say or do something reasonably unforgivable. If that was the case then he would have to wait a long time. Inside she was as lifeless and as empty of desire as a stone. The garden of unhappiness in which for all these years she had tended her private thoughts about Colin stood silent with neglect. She could not enter it; she felt estranged from those thoughts, yet they continued to exist, uncared for, seeding and sprawling and tangling up their shoots so that the well-planned lines of her disloyalty were slowly being erased. She did not blame Colin, as he lay there on the sofa with his thick white arms folded across his chest. It seemed to her that she had brought this ending on herself. She didn't know precisely when she had given herself over to opposition rather than to love; she knew only that she had balked at the loving, at the prospect of surrender.

Upstairs she draped herself in loose black silk and put on her silver necklace, which circled her throat with its cold clasp. She looked at herself in the mirror. Her face had the white density of marble. She felt all of a piece, heavy, heroic: she would go to the party alone if she had to. She said this to herself over and over as a means of navigating through the minutes, which narrowed towards six o'clock. Her heart knocked in her chest. Her hands shook as she coiled up her hair and pinned it to the top of her head. In this moment, facing the mirror with her arms lifted to her hair, she struck herself as beautiful. Unhappiness had scoured her out: it was as if a cast had been lifted from her, a thick, rough plaster of adult motivation. It was five to six. In this same moment she heard Colin's slow tread on the stairs and a flash of exultation and misery bolted across her chest. He entered the room behind her.

'When are we leaving?' he said.

She did not reply, but clipped earrings to her lobes. Their mean pinch was the pinch of the old life. Colin sighed, audibly.

'You don't have to come,' she said. 'I can go on my own quite easily.'

Colin said nothing. He started to unbutton his jeans and she looked away. When she looked again he was standing there in boxer shorts: he was all haunch and black fur. From where she stood she could just see the nest of hairs that grew in the hollow of his back. The sight of these hairs reminded her that Colin was unique. Most of the time she apprehended him as a generalised maleness – he was like a fog through which she could only ever see a few feet ahead. He cloaked his pudgy shoulders with a clean white shirt and began to do up the buttons. She felt that she had missed the opportunity of his nakedness, to understand him. His skin had reproached her for remote failures, which seemed to be failures of creativity. Colin had been a baby once; it struck her, standing before the mirror, that it was as a mother that she had failed him. She would have loved that baby's body, would have owned it, as she owned the bodies of her boys. But instead the physical fact of Colin, of Colin as a man, represented an irreparable difference, a breach. It was, almost, because he wasn't her child that she couldn't accept him. He was the outsider, the unwanted one. These thoughts caused her to pity Colin, so that she felt as though she might go to him and put her arms around him, as she did her children. Yet she did not; those thousand instances in which she had been summoned by her children's irresistible bodies, when she had been overridden by love, flogged out of her tiredness or disaffection by her bottomless loyalty to them, rose up in a great wall before her. Her power to refuse Colin seemed sometimes like the only power she had. She picked up a bottle of perfume and sprayed it at herself. Its cold mist settled on her neck, on her wrists. She looked in the mirror again and saw ice, glass, glittering concavities.

'Shall we walk?' she said to him, when the babysitter had come and they had put on their coats and left the boys flushed and indifferent in front of the television. Bidding them goodnight, Vanessa had felt no longer beautiful. She and Colin looked large and ridiculous, frumpy in their special clothes. Their disaffection protruded from each of them like a tail. Outside the front door, feeling the cold punch of the night air, seeing the sly glitter of stars, Vanessa cleaved to its hostile glamour. She didn't want to get in the car. The thought of them strapping in their ageing bodies repelled her. It seemed that a last dreg of promise lay somewhere at the bottom of the empty night. The snow, bluish, compacted, undulated around them like a ghostly ocean, like death. Colin, black and bulky in his overcoat, stood ahead of her down the path, his breath coming out in misty blooms.

'What?' he said.

'I just thought it would be nice to walk.'

He stood stock still with his back to her, his nose lifted slightly to the air. He held the car keys in his hand. There were moments in which Colin seemed already to be inhabiting a future that was not her future. Vanessa saw him as if in her own absence. The world moved away from her, sealed, like a missed train.

'I'd rather drive,' he said.

She was sitting out in the garden when she read that Victor had died. The summer was turning out hot. Every day she set a chair in the shade of the beech tree behind the house and listened to the sound the warm wind made in the leaves, and watched behind closed eyelids the sunlight making underwater shapes. The air was so comfortable against her skin that it was almost sensationless. It was like a second infancy, she thought, after all that pain. On mornings such as these she had put her babies in the pram under this same tree and they had lain there watching the leaves and the light, extending their new limbs into the waiting world.

Victor's obituary took up half a page. The writer talked about his life and his work, but his fame as Serena's husband moved across it all like the sun across the moon. There was a picture of him, younger, sitting at a desk in a blurred room full of files. He was survived, it said, by his wife and his two daughters. Vanessa wept a few tears and wiped them away with the back of her hand.

Serena and Victor had gone back to London in the spring. There were new people in the pink house now, a retired couple who'd ripped everything out and put on a new roof of orange tiles that perched there like a jaunty, ugly hat. They'd wanted a new garden too: they'd been Colin's first customers. It was a fussy garden, full of paths and bowers and an ornamental fish pond. It had taken him months. He spoke sometimes of the gardens of his suburban childhood, eventful gardens that told a story, and how he'd loved their frantic perfection, their crazy order. He said his grandfather had been a great gardener, a maker of rockeries and winter interest. The quintessential Englishman, he said. Colin drove a van with his name printed on the side. They'd bought it with some of the insurance money from Vanessa's accident. In the mornings he put the boys in it and drove them off to the nursery where they now spent half the day. Watching them go, the engine complaining as they met the hill, Vanessa would clutch her sides with panic but they always came back again, sailing down the lane on a wave of risk to eat their lunch in the kitchen. Vanessa could manage the boys in the afternoons now, but at first they had been away all day; and she still felt a strange homesickness for them, for the time before, when they had been close. She was getting stronger all the time. She was slowly filling with life. Yet she knew that she would never go back to her children: the mornings at nursery would remain, like a fence around her heart. That had been their decision, hers and Colin's. In those weeks when she had lain upstairs as cold and silent as a root in the hard winter ground, the world had steadily closed over the spaces she used to occupy. There were things to be done and Colin did them, not as she had done them but in his own way. When she got out of bed again she found that she had become unnecessary, and the fact of her continuing existence unfurled before her, blank, unmarked, full of possibility. She had looked in the mirror and she had not cried, in spite of the fact that she didn't recognise her own face. It was a new face, ugly, grateful, unable to disguise emotion. It was the face she had always suspected lay beneath the face she had before.

She'd got a letter from Kirsty that morning, the morning she read about Victor. Now that her eye was better she was having driving lessons, and when she could get in a car again she would go to Kirsty's prison and visit her. You could do that. She'd found out all about it. You could visit anyone who wanted to be visited. Vanessa felt she might have more to say to someone she didn't know than some-one she did, and she supposed people like Kirsty felt the same way. Kirsty spoke about her daughter in the letter. She was nearly two. She lived with foster parents who brought her to the prison every week. Vanessa was impressed by that. She wondered who these people were, who lived in the same world as her and yet were not the same. She wondered how they had come to be that way. It made her think about

Serena, and what Victor had once said about her being hard-hearted. She didn't think that was true. The other night she had seen her, on television, talking about the book she was publishing, a collection of all her columns, and something about the way the screen imprisoned her beautiful face told Vanessa how unhappy she was. She felt that she could almost see into her soul. The interviewer had asked her a question and while she listened a guard appeared to fall from her features; and for a second Vanessa saw her weeping, saw how deeply she believed herself to have done something bad and yet how she cleaved to it, to her success, her stories. She thought then that Victor must have hated the things Serena wrote, in spite of the fact that she wrote them for him. She wondered whether Serena believed that she'd killed Victor. She wondered whether that was what Colin believed, too, about the accident.

There in the sun she folded the newspaper so that Victor lay in the dark among the pages.